Much Curious Pleasure

Much Curious Pleasure

A NOVEL BY
JOHN
YEOMANS

ANGUS
& ROBERTSON
PUBLISHERS

*Creative writing programme assisted by
the Literature Board of the Australia Council,
the Federal Government's arts funding and
advisory body.*

ANGUS & ROBERTSON PUBLISHERS

*Unit 4, Eden Park, 31 Waterloo Road,
North Ryde, NSW, Australia 2113, and
16 Golden Square, London WIR 4BN,
United Kingdom*

*First published in Australia
by Angus & Robertson Publishers in 1987
First published in the United Kingdom
by Angus & Robertson (UK) in 1987*

Copyright © John Yeomans 1987

*National Library of Australia
Cataloguing-in-publication data.*

*Yeomans, John.
  Much curious pleasure.
  ISBN 0 207 15470 8.
  I. Title.*

A823'.3

*Typeset in 11pt English Times
Printed in Singapore*

To June, with love

1

After the morning parade, Reid and Jackson walked back to the old tent being used as the troop office. They were now the only two officers left in J troop; Shannahan had been killed and the professionally polite boy just out of Duntroon had been whisked to some staff job in Port Moresby.

'Half the men hadn't shaved,' Reid said. 'We must look like the bloody Yanks.'

'Razor blades are pretty short,' Jackson said.

'Everything seems short,' Reid grunted, flopping down in the tent on the bench beside the shabby table with collapsible metal legs which had travelled with the regiment from Australia to the Middle East and back to Australia and now to the island of Saruna. Jackson handed him a piece of paper with some faint typing on it, done on the troop's old Remington with the figure 2 missing. 'Ted wants this bumph back by 1200,' he said. 'Troop commanders to sign.'

'What is it this time? Return showing number and conditions of buckles on anklets web?'

'Return showing number of contact fuses. Docker counted our stuff.'

'And gave you his lecture on accurate returns, I'll bet,' said Reid. 'Where is he, anyway?'

'Took a working party down to the jetty to do some sort of repairs to it.'

'Christ, are we going to spend the rest of the war in this place?'

'Do it justice, Chris. Remember what Wilko said.'

Reid smiled and as always it infused an unexpected glow of warmth into his fair-skinned, clearly boned face, a face which often seemed to meet the world with a touch of hauteur.

'I know, I know,' he said. 'It keeps people away from their mothers-in-law. Give me the bloody pen.' He signed the return, put his hat on and said, 'I'm going to take a dutiful look at the gun position. See you at lunch, if that's the word for it.'

'Well, eat something,' said Jackson. 'You're looking pretty thin.' It was true. Reid's collar bones and knee joints seemed to be outlined within his jungle-green shirt and long pants.

'You sound like Zoe,' said Reid. 'In her last letter she asked how much I weighed and I wrote back to say I couldn't find the bathroom scales. Anyway, I'm off.'

As Reid walked away, the back of his shirt already showing the dark patch of sweat which even the slightest exertion caused in the merciless humidity, Jackson reflected that at least he could now hear Reid mention his wife without feeling he had to be on guard against something he might too-rapidly reply or even anything his face might reveal. He no longer had the sudden daytime fantasies which had maddened him when the troop had arrived on the island, but sometimes in his tent at night he still had a mental picture of Zoe in some shameless attitude. Bugger you, old Shanny boy, Jackson thought, checking the total on the ammunition return, if the Nips hadn't got you, Reid would still be in K Troop instead of here in J Troop with me; at least we don't share a tent, thank God. He picked up the return and began to walk, slowly, towards Battery HQ; the duty runner had gone sick that morning.

At lunchtime Jackson plodded over to the officers' mess, which was merely one of the group of gable tents, grey with age and travel, in which lived the Battery HQ and the two troops which made up 82 Battery. The tents were scattered about on the coarse grass between rows of regularly spaced coconut palms with grey-ringed trunks; almost all the tiny island had been a copra plantation before the war. The battery's eight 25-pounder field guns were deployed in two defensive positions on the edge of clearings several hundred yards away.

Jackson found Wilkinson, the battery commander, alone at the mess table, which was made of two office tables pushed together. There was no cloth.

'Where's everybody?' Jackson asked, surprised.

'Jack's at the airstrip trying to scrounge something, Athol is sick and the rest are at the hospital getting a lecture from some great expert on how the troops should take Atebrin,' Wilkinson said.

'You're kidding!'

'You'll find out,' said Wilkinson. 'You and Chris have to go tomorrow.' He put his head out of the tent and yelled. 'Come on, Whacker, are you trying to starve us?'

Wilkinson was a merry, nuggety, freckly man in his early thirties, who before the war had drifted from one pointless job to another, selling second-hand cars, running a hardware shop. The war had revealed his true vocation — he was an instinctive soldier. He had been a sergeant in a militia unit in 1939 and, having been almost immediately commissioned in the AIF, he rose rapidly to the rank of major in the explosive expansion of the Australian forces. The men liked and admired him. He had won a Military Cross in the Middle East and it was clear that if nothing happened to him he would go on to a much higher rank.

Whacker Davis, the batman rostered as mess orderly, came into the tent with a couple of dixies and put them on the rickety stand made of ammunition boxes in the corner of the tent.

'Afternoon, gents,' he said. 'Hope you've got a good appetite.' Davis was a big, raw-boned, ex-shearer who, to the battery's amazement, had asked to be taken off his gun to become Wilkinson's batman. It turned out that this gave him more time to run his evening two-up game which had become big business; it attracted men from all the nearby units including American Air Force ground crews who, cursing monotonously and barely comprehensibly, gambled great handfuls of dollars. Davis was putting portions of a grim stew on two enamel plates when Reid came into the tent and flopped down on a bench.

'My God, it's sticky today,' he said. He took off his hat and revealed an incongruous strip of white forehead above cheeks which, although very fair in complexion, had been well browned by the sun. Some men who wore hats all the time looked, without them, as though they were halfway through making up to play Othello.

'Guns OK?' Jackson asked.

'Buffer's leaking again on Number 2,' Reid said. 'How many times have we had an artificer look at that?'

Wilkinson laughed.

'I reckon tiffies are like plumbers. They like to keep coming back. What about some tea, Whacker?'

'Coming up right now, sir,' said Davis. He poured three cups of black tea from a kettle and put a tin of Carnation milk on the table. Jackson noticed that Reid, who had eaten only a couple of mouthfuls of the stew, took a sip of his tea and grimaced.

'How much chlorine are they putting in the water?' he asked. 'This tea tastes like a chemical experiment.'

Wilkinson, sipping the tea with apparent enjoyment, said, 'You on for a little slither tonight, Chris?'

Like all closed communities, the 82 Battery mess had developed private family words. A slither was a game of poker, a slather a game of pontoon, but nobody could remember how the words had originated. For inscrutable reasons, sometimes pontoon was the game played for a couple of weeks on end and then it would be replaced by poker. Normally one or other game was played three or four nights a week for reasonably high stakes in the mess tent, by the light of two petrol pressure lanterns.

'Not tonight, thanks, Tim,' said Reid. 'I must write a couple of letters.' He stood up, nodded to everybody and walked away.

Wilkinson looked after him and remarked, 'Our Christopher doesn't look the best. Not getting malaria, is he, George?'

'I think he's bored,' Jackson said.

'Jesus, who isn't?' said Wilkinson. 'I'd rather be at Randwick myself.'

'I don't mind being bored for a bit,' Jackson said. 'It makes a nice change after the recent episode.'

'Some men take boredom better than others,' Wilkinson said. 'Don't they, Whacker?'

'Tell 'em to come down to the swy game, sir,' Davis said. 'If they win a few bob it might cheer them up.'

'I don't want to hear about your illegal activities. What about washing this tent? It's filthy.' Wilkinson swung as easily as ever from informality to command, as he was able to do with all ranks in his battery; Jackson envied him this not very common military gift.

'I'll round up a couple of other batmen and we'll do it this arvo,' Davis promised.

Wilkinson finished his tea and stood up.

'Well, I've got to go to Brigade to hear the wisdom from on high,' he told Jackson, and walked away whistling. Davis collected the plates and dixies and strolled off. Jackson, finishing his tea, ran his eye idly around the tent; it could certainly do with a wash. Suddenly he noticed, in one corner, a three-cornered tear which had been crudely mended. Good God! Jackson thought. This is the tent that was used as the battery office when the Japs landed — I remember seeing that tear when Wilko gave us the briefing.

Jackson moved over and reminiscently ran his hand over the tear; it had been mended with what seemed like ordinary string. He looked slowly around the rest of the tent, trying to recognise some other identifying marks but he could see none. Where had he himself stood during the briefing? Somewhere in the middle of the group of officers, he vaguely recalled. Then his ears noticed a sound which had become so common that ordinarily he did not register it; it was the scream of a Kittyhawk engine pushed to full revolutions as the plane, taking off, raced down the airstrip out of sight nearly a mile away. Jackson, head cocked, waited for what he knew was coming next and the scream

5

duly died to a rumble as the plane became airborne and the pilot throttled back. Those were the sounds repeated at intervals of only a few moments he had heard as he and Shannahan had walked over for the briefing.

2

It had been 1500 hours when Wilkinson had sent runners around with an order for all officers to report to him in the battery office immediately. It was only two days since the ancient freighter which had collected 82 Battery in Broome had dumped it on the rickety wooden jetty which seemed to form the port of Saruna. The guns and vehicles were still scattered through the trees near the wharf.

In the tent, the officers found Wilkinson looking pre-occupied. He usually started a briefing with a joke, but now he was carefully reading what he had written in his note-book.

'Are we all here?' he asked. 'Good. Well, gentlemen, I have just returned from a conference of all unit commanders with the brigadier commanding the island. I don't have to tell you that since the fall of Singapore the Japanese have stead-ily driven south and are at this moment fighting our troops in New Guinea. There seems little doubt that the Japanese High Command envisages an attack on the Australian main-land and that gives importance to the otherwise insignificant piece of real estate on which we are now standing. The airstrip on Saruna is used by both the American Air Force and the RAAF and if this fell into Japanese hands it would give their planes a base from which to attack Darwin. That is why our battery was sent up here in such haste — to help protect the airstrip.'

'Haste is right,' somebody muttered.

Wilkinson nodded.

'It was intended that the other two batteries of the regiment and some more infantry were to be sent in a second convoy but it is doubtful whether this can now reach us in time, or at all.'

He glanced at his notebook and went on briskly, 'Half an hour ago, I and other unit commanders were warned by the brigadier that at first light this morning our air patrols sighted a Japanese naval force, including ships equipped with landing barges, in the Banda Sea.'

'Heading this way?' asked Shannahan.

'Apparently so. It is assumed their intention is to make a landing here on Saruna.'

Jackson realised with astonishment that there was every likelihood that he would shortly be in combat with the Japanese and he felt a great hand close around his stomach and squeeze it; this physical, exactly located reaction to fear was new to him. He glanced furtively around the faces of the other officers; they looked impassive, sustained by past experience. He felt more of an outsider than ever, for he alone of the officers in the tent had not been in action in the Middle East or North Africa.

Wilkinson was speaking again.

'All units are to take up defensive positions immediately. Brigade's problem is to make a very small force go around and this battery is therefore to defend the area around the jetty in case the Japanese simply drive up and try to land barges at the beaches beside it. Shanny — J Troop will deploy in a line across the beach on the left of the wharf. Eric — K Troop is to do the same on the beach on the right. The guns are to be placed just back from the sand so they can fire over open sights at landing craft.'

There was a rustle of surprise among the officers. It seemed absurd to be talking seriously of using a machine capable of hitting a target more than seven miles distant to blaze away at something two hundred yards off. Wilkinson looked around the group with a twinkle of grim amusement in his eyes.

'Some of us have never done a shoot over open sights, I'll bet. Better have a squint at the gun drill book before dark,' he said. 'I want the guns deployed and phone lines

8

established at once. All the information I have given you is to be passed on to the troops. And there's one thing I'd like you to impress on the men —'

He folded his notebook shut and put it into his shirt pocket.

'Saruna is an island. Our air force is certainly dominant in this area but the Japanese Navy has fairly full control of the sea. We were lucky our own ship managed to sneak in, and our chance of being reinforced now is very slim indeed. If the Japanese do land, we will have to fight it out to a finish here because there's no chance our own navy will be able to take us off. That's all for the moment. I will inspect the gun positions from 1800 onwards. Any questions — no? Carry on, gentlemen.'

In the silence the Battery Captain said 'Up!' and the officers' right arms swung upwards in a simultaneous salute. The formality seemed appropriate. As the officers filed out of the tent several winked at each other with a little sideways dip of the head; Jackson knew it was one of the battery's private family jokes, meaning, 'That's telling 'em!', and used as a sly silent comment after the issue of some remarkable order.

As an untried reinforcement officer he had never dared to do it. He hung back until he could attach himself to Shannahan, his troop commander, and left the tent walking a pace behind him. Shannahan, striding purposefully away through the coconut palms towards J Troop, suddenly laughed. 'Bloody open sights!' he said. 'We could throw a few tins of bully at them, too. One of those cans would give a Nip a nasty knock.'

He seemed to be enjoying himself; his green eyes which slanted like a cat's were shining. Shannahan dug Jackson in the ribs. 'Christ!' he said. 'You might be an old digger soon!'

Jackson was twenty-two and Shannahan was only twenty-five. Jackson was as tall as Shannahan and more solidly built. Unlike the ebullient Shannahan, Jackson, olive-skinned and dark-haired, always seemed to think before he spoke. Strangers often took him to be twenty-six or twenty-seven. But as he walked back to the troop with Shannahan he felt like a child trotting beside his father to his first day at school, anticipating what was to come with a mixture of curiosity and dread.

3

The four guns of J Troop and its little flock of vehicles were still under the trees to which they had been dispersed after they had bumped off the jetty. The rusty Dutch cargo ship which had brought the troop from Broome had scuttled out to sea the moment the sweating working parties had pulled the last case of ammunition and rations out of the holds. The gaunt, cheroot-smoking captain who had escaped from Batavia, but had been forced to leave his wife and three children behind, knew there was a chance he might run into a prowling Japanese destroyer as he tried to dodge back to the mainland, but he had no wish to be a sitting target tied up to a jetty. Some J Troop gunners and signallers were still sorting out stores when Shannahan told Docker, the Troop Sergeant Major, to fall in the men. Shannahan told them exactly what Wilkinson had told the officers. Again the news was heard in a profound silence; glancing down the ranks, Jackson saw the faces set in frowns of concentration, the sun-hardened eyes reduced to slits under the eyebrows.

'We are going to move the guns at once,' Shannahan said. 'Mr Jackson is staying here. Sergeant Major Docker and I are leaving for the beach immediately. The TSM will come back and lead the guns to the beach. I will meet them there and site them individually. Numbers One — I want tractors hooked on and crews mounted in half an hour. We will bring down personal gear later today. Any questions?'

'Excuse me, sir — ' said Docker.

It would be Docker, obstructionist bastard, Jackson thought.

'What about rations, sir?' Docker asked.

It was a pointless question, but Shannahan answered patiently. 'We'll arrange all that when the guns are in. Get the men moving now.'

'Very good, sir,' Docker said in the disapproving tone he used when he was not listened to at length. He swung around in a theatrical about-turn and as usual had to take a little step afterwards to recover his balance; the men mercilessly imitated this.

'J Troop — you have heard your duties!' Docker shouted, unnecessarily. 'J Troop, break off!' The men all did a quiet little right turn, paused for the regulation moment and clustered around the gun sergeants. In five minutes everybody had slipped away to a gun or a vehicle. Shannahan jumped into his one-ton truck and disappeared down the road to the beach. Docker climbed on his motorcycle and managed to start it after four kicks; he was a tall, bony man, who crouched uneasily on the machine as though he disapproved of that, too.

An hour and a half later, all four guns were in position in a staggered line along the grass verging on the sand of the beach to the left of the jetty, their shields down and their barrels depressed to horizontal. Jackson, as the J Troop Gun Position Officer, had sited his command post, still merely a pile of gear and two telephones, on the wet grass a little further back. The signallers were running a wire to the battery command post somewhere up the road. Shannahan was in high spirits.

'Lawks a-mercy,' he said, grinning. 'We'll see the Light Brigade charge past in a minute. Now, here's the drill. Each gun is to keep one up the spout and twenty rounds behind the trail. Two of the crew are to be on the gun in two-hour watches all night and you and I and Docker will do two-hour watches as look-outs. As a matter of fact, I reckon we should have a couple of blokes as lookouts on the end of the jetty as well, with a Very pistol or a phone or something to let us know if they see or hear any barges. Why don't you duck over the road and arrange with Chris Reid that each troop will supply men in alternate watches or something?'

Something inside Jackson shrank, as it did before every meeting, or even the prospect of a meeting, with Christopher Reid, who as the Gun Position Officer of the other troop in the battery was his operational opposite number.

'To tell you the truth, Shanny,' Jackson said. 'I would like to get the command post organised first —'

'You do that,' said Shannahan. 'I'll duck over and see Chris in a minute.' He looked at the jetty, still visible in the last of the afternoon sun. 'Christ, what a rickety old thing. Looks as though it might collapse if we put a couple of heavyweights out there.' He clapped Jackson on the shoulder. 'Your bridge-building school didn't extend to jetty repairs, did it?'

Jackson took a slow breath before he answered. It was a small foolish trick he had adopted, believing that it saved him from saying anything unguarded whenever the school was mentioned.

'I expect that jetty is beyond repair,' Jackson said.

Docker came up and gave an uncalled-for salute. 'Excuse me, sir —' he began.

'OK, OK,' said Shannahan jovially. 'What's gone wrong?'

'Well, sir, you know we don't have any armour piercing ammunition, don't you? We don't even have enough untorn mosquito nets to go around. I'd say we are going to get our first malaria cases pretty soon.'

'We've got our Atebrin, though, haven't we?' Shannahan asked. 'Those essential little yellow tablets, eh?'

'We've got those, but not all the men have long-sleeved shirts. They rush the unit up here six weeks after we get back from the Middle East and then try to work out what gear we should have — it's all arse versus science as usual.'

'It is indeed,' said Shannahan. 'All the best amateur armies are run this way.'

Docker pursed his lips. 'Very amateur,' he said. He was one of the few regular soldiers in the regiment; before the war he had been an acting sergeant in an ordnance depot, which had been a generous reward for his military talents, but the war in its mysterious way had catapulted him to warrant rank in a combat unit, which he never ceased to criticise.

'You know the vehicles are still fitted with sand tyres, don't you?' he said. 'I don't think the tractors will be able to move the guns if it rains much more.'

Jackson and Shannahan both knew this was true. The regiment was equipped with superb British 25-pounder field guns (so called because that was the weight of the shell) but they were towed by antediluvian high-sided Marmon Herrington tractors which were in fact not tracked but tyred. They had a four-wheel drive which threw out of gear when the steering was on full lock and as gun movers they were ideal for a gentlemanly skirmish in Mesopotamia. But Shannahan, determined not to be drawn, merely clapped Docker on the shoulder and said, 'Well, don't worry. We're not going anywhere tonight.'

Jackson took first watch. The darkness fell with tropical suddenness, but an almost full moon came up; the coconut plantation behind the guns became a sorcerer's wood and the blue-black water stretched in limitless mystery before them. A little wind made the palm leaves rustle, but the air was warm; the moonlight was so theatrically bright that the guns cast hard-edged shadows on the ground and metal objects such as the range cones on the dial sights sparkled. The mosquitoes whined spitefully around. Men not on watch, warned to keep their trousers tucked into their socks and stay under the nets rigged from ropes between the trees, were supposed to be getting some sleep, but most of them were too tense for that. Shannahan had his truck and Jackson's placed at the extreme ends of the line of guns so their headlights could be turned on in an emergency. Everybody spoke in whispers as though the Japanese might hear them.

'Bloody comical, isn't it?' said Shannahan, materialising beside Jackson. 'The artillery is in the front line on the beach and the infantry is behind us in the trees. If the Japs land, we'll get a bullet up the bum, too.'

He laughed to himself, his teeth gleaming white in the moonlight. Jackson felt a surge of affection for this tall, happy man who wore an absurd, carefully cultivated Battle of Britain air force moustache. Captain Shannahan came of an Irish family and loved to make terrible jokes about the Catholic church. He did not claim much academic knowledge of the science of gunnery but he was an excellent practical troop commander and the men, liking him, had long ago nicknamed him Shanny Boy. Before the war he had been a salesman for a roofing company.

'I think I'll have a natter to the crews,' he said. He strode away, clearly visible until he was almost at Number 4 gun. He seemed tireless. Jackson raised his binoculars again, and stared into the blue haze which covered the water beyond the beach and gradually thickened to an impenetrable blackness. He turned his head from side to side listening for whatever previously-never-heard sound a Japanese landing barge engine might make, but all he heard was the faint swish-swish of wavelets no more than a couple of inches high breaking on the sand. He raised his glasses again and in them saw Zoe Reid. She was sitting beside him, on the sofa, the afternoon they ate the scorched almonds.

Jackson quickly dropped the glasses, but he was helpless as his mental monitor rescreened what had happened that day in her house in Wahroonga.

He remembered how angular and strong-jawed her face had looked when, giving him one of her strange smiles, she had slewed around on the sofa to face him and leaned back to allow her shoulders to rest on the arm at the end of the sofa. Then, saying nothing but looking at him quizzically, she had slowly raised her right leg and placed it on his left shoulder. He had seen her dress slip down her bare brown leg and realised she was wearing nothing under it. She had put both hands behind his head and pulled it down into the aromatic mat of wiry black hair between her legs. 'Go on,' she had said, arching her back to push her pubic bone hard against his face, 'Go on!'

On the beach at Saruna, Jackson gave a half-groan of distress. He had not thought about Zoe all day until then and now the all-too-clear recollection of the sexual gymnastics into which she had led him on that sofa threatened to flood his mind. 'No, bugger it!' Jackson said, aloud, as he felt himself stiffening in his slacks. He fell back on a trick he had devised, to ward off Zoe when she became too vivid; he imagined that his mental screen was being cleared by a movie-type wipe and so the beach and guns slid on to it from the right and pushed Zoe off to the left.

Jackson walked over to the Number 3 gun, anxious to talk to somebody quickly. The gun sergeant, a hawk-nosed dairy farmer with a mention in dispatches, muttered a greeting. The other man on the gun was a delicate-looking boy who was, Jackson recalled, an art student in civil life. Suppose a line of Japanese barges did come charging in, Jackson wondered ... will the men keep loading, aiming and firing? Army discipline is designed to produce men who continue to obey orders even when they are frightened and confused — does it? And what about me? What does discipline do for a shit-scared lieutenant with a guilty conscience?

4

It was not, after all, at the little port that the Japanese landed; they came ashore two nights later three miles away, at the top of the island. The Kittyhawks flying reconnaissance missions from the Saruna strip saw the barges on the beaches in the dawn, but the troops had disappeared beneath the roof of the coconut palm foliage which covered ninety per cent of the island. The sand seemed to have been brushed over as though to conceal the marks of whatever wheeled or tracked equipment had come ashore, but if the Japanese had brought troop carriers or light tanks it was obvious they would have to come down the only road leading from the top of the island through the plantations to the jetty. The Australian brigadier commanding the defence of Saruna therefore swung his troops across the road in a half circle and ordered Wilkinson to get his guns off the beach into positions from which they could give support fire to the forward infantry units. The eight guns of 82 Battery were the defenders' total field artillery.

All spare bodies, including the cooks and the clerks, were set to work with such axes as were available to hack down the trees on the edges of some clearings, enlarging them so the guns could lift their projectiles over the top branches. It rained heavily while this was going on and the tractors barely managed to move the guns through the mud.

The Japanese attackers, it was realised soon enough, were remarkably unlike the buck-toothed bespectacled little apes of Allied propaganda. The ones who landed on Saruna were the muscular, elite marines of a Special Landing Party, whose morale had been well bolstered by the knowledge that 60 000 Japanese had taken prisoner 120 000 British, Australian, Indian and Malayan troops after the fall of Singapore in one of the most humiliating defeats in British military history. The Japanese on Saruna did not unsportingly bring pushbikes like those on which they had infiltrated the Malayan plantations. They merely waited until nightfall and then set off to march in a body down the road leading to the Saruna jetty. It was never discovered why they landed so far up the coast when a doorstep landing opposite the airstrip might have led to its immediate capture. Despite later theories which credited their commander with devilish but obscure cunning, the truth may simply be that the Japanese Navy made a mistake and put the landing party down at the wrong place. At any rate, the marines marched down the road, making no attempt at silence (as Australian troops attested in bewilderment later) but talking, laughing and even singing.

If they did this to draw fire and quickly discover where the Australian outposts were, they soon succeeded. The first Australian to challenge them was a lance corporal in a CMF battalion deployed across the road. He was a nineteen-year-old former garage boy who, hearing a group of men clumping towards him in the dark of the roadway, stepped out from behind the tree where he had been smoking, for some reason brought his rifle up to the regulation 'On Guard', as he had done so often during drill, and shouted, 'Halt! Who goes there?' The Japanese chopped him down with a couple of submachine gun bursts, the boy's companions fled back down the track and the Japanese spread out off the road to probe the Australian defences.

By noon next day there had been no further contact with the Japanese, who were obviously organising themselves for some sort of push. The brigadier deployed a company of an AIF battalion, which had already fought both at El Alamein and in New Guinea, across the roadway and J Troop was ordered to support this company. K Troop was deployed in support of other companies guarding the coastal flank. The malaria which caused more casualties than gunshot wounds among Allied troops in the Pacific campaigns was already eating into 82 Battery. A J Troop driver and a signaller, shivering uncontrollably and drenched in sweat, had stumbled away to the field hospital set up in a plantation hut. In the dusk Shannahan went up to the infantry position so that he could direct the fire of the guns from there as a forward observation officer the next day. He did not take both a signaller and an Observation Post Assistant but only his OPA, at that time an acting bombardier (artillery corporal) named Richards, aged eighteen, who was also to man the phone carrying Shannahan's fire orders down to the gun position.

At first light next morning the phone cable, the last part of which had been laid by Shannahan and Richards, was soon busy. Shannahan registered four targets by firing sufficient rounds to establish the line, range and angle of sight to spots on which future fire could be called down in a hurry. Jackson, shouting the fire orders to the guns through his old megaphone, knew Shannahan was using the procedure for engaging targets so close to the observation post that, for fear of hitting himself, the observer abandoned the usual long bracket, short bracket drill and crept the fire down towards himself in cautious fifty or even twenty-five-yard steps. Jackson tried to picture where Shanny was, but it was as though he had disappeared through the looking glass into another world.

Finally Shannahan came on the phone himself. 'Keep one gun laid on each of the targets I've registered,' he said. 'Keep a round up the spout in each one and have somebody ready to grab the firing handle.'

'Where are you?' Jackson asked.

'I'm with the infanteers on our side of a clearing in the plantation. There's a theory that the Nips are just on the other side — the four spots I've registered are over there.'

'Be nice if we had some proper maps,' Jackson said. All he and Shannahan had were two copies of a pen and ink sketch-map of the island run off on a duplicator somewhere.

'Be better if we had some cold Reschs,' said Shannahan. 'I'll send you a postcard later.'

Then followed a nerve-stretching two days in which rumours of Japanese probes and clashes with Australian patrols filtered in over the phone system but no attack developed. 'Bloody odd,' Shannahan said over the phone, sounding tired. 'The infanteers reckon this spot where I am is a very likely place for the little bastards to have a go and they're sure there are Nips on the other side of the clearing, but I haven't seen one.'

Wilkinson went up to the clearing that afternoon and next day he ordered Jefferson, the young regular just out of Duntroon who had been acting as a section officer in K Troop, to take over as J Troop's Gun Position Officer. Shannahan was to come back to the guns for a rest and Jackson was to go up to the infantry in his place.

'I'm to relieve you at 1600,' Jackson told Shannahan. He did not add that the thought of taking over the forward observation post terrified him.

'OK,' said Shannahan. 'It's not far to walk.'

At half past three Jackson and Rodgers, his bombardier Command Post Assistant, a phlegmatic bank clerk, collected their gear and set off to walk up the white dirt road still rutted by the wheels of the trucks which used to rattle up and down it carrying copra. It seemed absurd to Jackson that this was the way you went to the front, walking through a coconut plantation. At first it seemed deserted but soon they passed a couple of infantrymen sitting on a log, looking after a phone maintenance terminal. They nodded to Jackson, but said nothing. When he came to a bend in the track, he saw a biggish clearing ahead and a voice hissed. 'Get off the road, you silly buggers — they're just on the other side of the clearing.' Jackson, surprised, dodged behind a tree trunk and saw that a couple of sections of infantry were in shallow trenches near him. They looked noticeably alert.

'You from the arty?' asked a corporal. 'Your officer's up there with our skipper. Follow your phone wire, but you'd better crawl. They've got a sniper who knocked off one of our blokes half an hour ago.'

Jackson, his stomach frozen now to a solid block, saw the artillery phone cable running forward through the trees. He dropped on his face and began to pull himself forward on elbows and knees; his binoculars and revolver dug painfully into his body. Raising his head, he saw Shannahan, Richards and another man crouching in a shallow hollow scooped in the earth behind the horizontal trunk of a chopped-down palm tree on the edge of the clearing. Still ten yards away, Jackson called to Shannahan who waved to him to come forward. Jackson crawled up beside him.

'What ho, Malvolio!' said Shannahan. 'For this relief much thanks.'

'G'day,' said the other man who was, Jackson realised, the infantry company commander. 'I'm Ted Salisbury.' He and Jackson shook hands. Salisbury was an angular, blond captain in his twenties.

'Where are the Nips?' Jackson asked, feeling flustered and absurdly green. He went to peer over the big log, but the captain pulled him back.

'There's no doubt where the little bastards are now,' he said. 'They're in the trees over there, so keep your head down.'

'Show me your map,' Shannahan said.

Lying awkwardly on one side, Jackson struggled to pull his mapboard to where he could see it. 'I reckon the guns are here,' Shannahan said, jabbing at a spot on the pen and ink sketch. 'And we are about here, I hope. The zero line is forty-seven degrees, which I earnestly trust runs through the middle of this clearing.'

Jackson, feeling the sweat running into his eyes, said, 'Where did you register those targets?'

'I reckon here, here, here and here,' said Shannahan, pointing to four crosses neatly numbered on his map. 'They are places on the far edge of the clearing where Ted here reckons the Japs would be likely to form up for a charge. I had to be bloody careful about creeping down — the fifty per cent zone for this range is not too big, thank God, but I had the shits the whole time in case a funny one dropped down my own neck.'

'Can you actually see any of the points you registered?' Jackson asked.

'You can see the most important one,' said Shannahan. 'This cart track we're on goes right across the clearing and beside it on the other side there's an old machine of some sort lying on the grass. You can see it pretty clearly, actually —'

Shannahan wriggled forward on his elbows and, raising his binoculars to his eyes, put his head around the end of the log. Jackson was on the point of wriggling forward to lie beside him when a single shot rang out and a hairy caterpillar a couple of inches long landed on his map. Staring at it, puzzled, Jackson saw that the caterpillar had blond hair on its back, but its sides and bottom were red.

'Oh, Jesus,' said Richards, 'Captain Shannahan's been hit!'

5

'Pull him back,' said the infantry officer.

He and Jackson pulled Shannahan behind the log. Blood was pouring out of quite a small red hole above Shannahan's right eye, but one side of the back of his head was a pulpy mass of blood and a spongy material which Jackson realised incredulously was some of Shannahan's brain. The caterpillar which had landed on his mapboard had been a piece of skull with the hair attached.

'That fucking Nip is up a tree somewhere,' said the infantry officer. 'They love to do that.' He called quietly back to the group of men behind him. 'Jack, tell the flank section to look up the trees on the right of the clearing — that sniper is there somewhere.'

Shannahan was making gurgling sounds through his hideously open mouth. Jackson and Rodgers frantically pressed field dressings on his wounds but by this time the grass beneath Shannahan's head had changed from a bright red to a darker red and then to a brown, so that it looked as though somebody had drained a car sump there. Yet Shannahan still made little moaning sounds; Jackson wondered how the human body could continue like this when half the brain had been blown away.

'Hey, skipper . . .' called a voice from behind the next log. 'Bill Freebody reckons he can see a Nip up a tree. Could be the cunt who got the arty bloke.'

'Tell Ted to take his time and see if he can bring the bastard down,' said the captain. Shannahan made a snoring sound and his whole body convulsed. The small denture he wore had fallen down across his tongue. Thinking it might go down his throat, Jackson forced himself to put his hand in Shannahan's mouth and hooked the bridge out with his forefinger. He remembered how Shannahan used to joke about his little plate ('wonderful piece of craftsmanship — I only take it out to eat') and he suddenly felt like crying.

'We've got to get him out of here and back to an MO,' he said. Jackson knelt up to take Shannahan around the shoulders and was roughly pulled down by the infantry officer.

'Turn it up,' he said. 'The bloody Nip will get you too if you stand up.'

'But we must get him back — I think he's still breathing.'

'I don't think he is,' said the captain. 'And, anyway, he can't be moved for the moment. Use your nut.'

Jackson fell back on the ground feeling helpless. A slow fusillade of shots from the Australian .303 rifles rang out from somewhere off to the right and a little later the sergeant of the section behind them called out, 'Hey, skipper, Bill Freebody passed a message. He thinks he hit a Nip up a tree near that old cart or whatever it is over there. Can you see anything from where you are?'

'I'll take a look,' said Salisbury.

Jackson saw Bombardier Richards glance at him and glance quickly away.

'No, fuck that!' Jackson said, seizing Salisbury's arm. 'I'll look — he was our bloke.'

'We'll both look,' said Salisbury. 'You go down to the other end of the log and keep your glasses down near the ground.'

Jackson, steeling himself, crawled down, and heart in mouth, put his face far enough out from behind the log to get his eyes to the binoculars. They instantly steamed over. Cursing, he elbowed backwards, wiped the lenses with his handkerchief, and put his head out around the end of the log again. Before the lenses steamed over again he saw a man hanging head down from the top branches of a palm tree. He was suspended by one foot apparently tied to the trunk.

Jackson pulled himself back and described what he had seen.

'I saw him, too,' said Salisbury. 'Tied himself to the tree so he could go on shooting even if he got hit himself. The Nips used to do that in New Guinea; they all want to die for the emperor.'

From the far side of the clearing there suddenly arose a hoarse chant. Salisbury looked quickly around the log.

'Jesus!' he said, rolling quickly back. His face had whitened underneath its tan.

'What's the matter?' asked Jackson.

'A mob of Nips is forming in the trees — I think they're getting ready to charge us.' In a loud voice he called out, 'B Company, stand to! The Nips may be coming at us. Bren gunners, are you ready? Don't fire until they come out in the open.'

Another burst of sound came across the clearing, this time half shouting, half screaming.

'That's it,' said the captain. He pulled his revolver out of its webbing holster. 'They'll take off in a minute. Well, come on, you arty blokes! Put some fucking rounds down — what are you here for?'

For a moment Jackson could not think what to do. Bombardier Rodgers reacted first; he grabbed the handset of the field telephone and put it up to his mouth.

'Shit!' called one of the infantrymen somewhere. 'They've got some of those little flags!'

'Give it to them!' the infantry captain said urgently to Jackson. 'Give it to them!'

Jackson's mind reactivated. Seizing the handset from Rodgers, he snapped, 'Targets 1, 2, 3 and 4, five rounds gunfire.' He paused from force of habit waiting for the report 'Ready' to come back from the guns and then realising the guns were already laid and loaded added, 'Fire!' The screaming on the other side of the clearing had become maniacal.

It seemed a long time but it was only a few seconds, because the gun position was not far behind them, before the men at the log heard the grunting woof, woof, woof, of four 25-pounders sending off twenty shells as fast as the layers could level the bubbles. Jackson huddled against Shannahan's body, pressing himself against the still-warm mass in the filthy jungle greens.

'Cover up,' he shouted to the others. He knew that although the range tables said that no shell should fall as far short as the log, any small error in gunlaying on such close targets might drop a round on the forward infantry positions. He tucked his head under his arms and was instantly ashamed of himself; his duty was to observe the fire. The first shells began crashing into the plantation, but the normal sound sequence seemed to have been perverted. The express-train rumblings of the shells in the air, the sharp explosion of the landed shells and the deep barking of the guns firing all seemed to be heard at the same time.

Jackson saw gobbets of smoke coming up from spots around the old piece of machinery. Then came an ear-splitting crack as a round landed in the clearing itself and there was a ghastly whistling and chopping sound as fragments of the shell casing tore through the palm leaves above the Australian infantry's heads. Jackson, looking in prolongation of the log, saw the flashes of shells exploding in the trees at one side of the clearing, too. Then somewhere near him he heard the interrupted blat-blat-blat of Bren guns being fired in bursts and then there was absolute silence.

'Christ,' said the infantry captain. 'I bet that rattled the little bastards.' He peered out around the end of the log. 'We got a few of them. I can see the bodies.' He turned his head and shouted, 'Good work, B Company!' A deep bushman's voice drawled back. 'And good on the arty. We knew the poofters would be useful sometime.'

Jackson saw the amusement on the captain's face. Much of the infantry regarded the artillery as an unduly formal branch of the Australian army; conversely artillery officers tended to disapprove when they met infantry platoons in which the privates called their lieutenant by his first name.

'Have you been in action before?' Salisbury asked.

Jackson shook his head.

'Well, you did all right,' said Salisbury. Jackson felt more than pride; exultation swept over him. At last he had crossed the great barrier between the innocent and the blooded and he thought, 'I'll be buggered! All that drill about registering targets actually worked.'

'What do you reckon the Nips will do now?' Richards asked.

'I'd say they're re-forming back in the trees to try again,' said Salisbury.

'Are they?' said Jackson. 'I know something that might change their minds. Rodgers — grab the phone. Fire orders. Registered targets, three rounds gunfire two oh seconds. Fire when ready.'

Again the storm of metal pieces slashed through the trees across the clearing, but now each gun's shells were spaced twenty seconds apart. Once the whole log shook as a fragment thudded loudly into the wood. Excitement flooded through Jackson. He felt like Jove commanding the thunderbolts. He had only to speak a few syllables to unleash hell among the flesh and bone sheltering on the other side of the clearing.

'That should drive them back a bit,' said Salisbury.

'How far back?'

'Hundred yards, couple of hundred yards, maybe.'

'We can accommodate them,' said Jackson. 'Stop,' he ordered. 'Up 200, three rounds gunfire two oh seconds, fire when ready.' The shells began bursting in the trees, 200 yards further into the plantation. When the noise and smoke died away, Jackson asked, 'Will they attack again?'

'They won't give up, that's for sure,' said the captain. 'They're tough bastards. Now they've been knocked back here they'll probably slip away and try and probe in some other place on our perimeter. That's what they did at Ghobu.' He nodded at Shannahan's body. 'We could get your mate out of here, if you like.'

Jackson looked at Shannahan. His eyes were half open in the sly glance of death.

27

'I'll get my blokes to carry him,' Salisbury said. Two privates crawled up and, crouching, ran with Shannahan's body back into the trees behind them.

Jackson called the GPO on the phone. 'Shanny has been killed,' he told Jefferson, abruptly.

Before Jefferson could reply, Jackson said, 'I'll tell you all about it later.' Then, slipping unconsciously into the calm assured tone of command, he went on, 'I want you to get the guns laid back on the original registered targets — take off the 200. Keep crews on the guns ready to fire at once until you hear further. Next, pass the message to Major Wilkinson that Shanny was killed during an attack by the Japanese on the B Company position at the forward observation post — you've got the spot on the map. And tell the major I'll stay in the OP here until I hear from him. Are you clear on that?'

'Very good, sir,' the boy answered. 'What ... was Shanny —'

'I'll tell you later. Get hold of Wilko now.'

The infantry captain came back. 'I've spoken to my CO on our phone,' he said. 'He's going to get C Company to send in a couple of patrols from the flank to see what's going on ahead of us.' He grimaced. 'Better them than us. We've put your mate beside the track down there. Your mob could get a vehicle up tonight.'

Twenty minutes later Wilkinson came on the phone, speaking briskly and concisely. 'I am dreadfully sorry about Shanny,' he said. 'He was a man I liked and a good officer. And I know that you did well up there.'

'I did nothing,' Jackson said. 'Nothing. Shanny set up the targets and I just fired on them blind. It was Shanny's ...' He felt his voice beginning to tremble and he coughed quickly to hide it. 'It was Shanny's shoot.'

'And yours, George,' said Wilkinson. 'And yours.' His voice went crisp again. 'I'll arrange to have the body collected and you can tell me the details later. Meantime, you are to continue to man the OP. I think young Jefferson had better stay with the guns so I'll switch Reid from K Troop to

28

relieve you tomorrow. He'll be up an hour before dark.'

Reid arrived punctually with his own assistant and crawled up behind the log, looking extraordinarily clean. Jackson and the bombardiers left him talking to Salisbury, for whom there seemed to be no relief. They retreated through the trees and began walking down the dirt road leading towards the rear. Incredible, thought Jackson, I walked up to the war and now I'm walking away from it, like a mechanic doing shift work at a power station. Then Shannahan said to him, 'Bloody awful having to work from these maps.' And Jackson answered, 'Better than nothing, Shanny.'

'What's that, sir?' asked Richards.

'I didn't say anything,' Jackson told him, surprised.

They plodded on. Jackson several times heard Shannahan's voice, clear, normal, relaxed, talking about troop business. Once he spoke about Annette's place in Cairo. The voice was so loud Jackson almost imagined the bombardiers could hear it. Much later he mentioned it to a doctor, who told him it was a not-uncommon phenomenon of exhaustion, but Jackson remembered for the rest of his life how clearly Shannahan had talked to him after he was dead.

Next day Wilkinson told him that Reid, as the senior subaltern in the battery, would take over J Troop as its commander. It was a normal posting; Reid was soon due for a captaincy, anyway.

'Do I stay?' Jackson asked Wilkinson.

'Sure; you and Reid get along OK, don't you?'

'Oh, yes,' said Jackson. 'Yes, of course.'

6

A week later, after the Japanese had attacked in several places and been driven back, and after J Troop had moved its guns up and back and fired at targets seemingly all over the island, Jefferson was on duty as Gun Position Officer, Reid was Forward Observation Officer and Jackson, soon to relieve him, was trying to sleep in the stifling heat, lying on top of his valise beneath his net, when he heard the rustle of some nocturnal creature in the grass near him and he recalled immediately the lizards at Wahroonga. He groaned aloud and rolled over trying to turn out the light on his mental screen but it was useless; once again he was walking up the little track which led through the tree-covered vacant block of land behind Christopher and Zoe Reid's house.

Zoe had shown him this path when they became lovers; after a day at the bridge-building school Jackson used to park his old car a couple of streets away and walk through the empty block, slip through a gap in the paling fence and, hidden by a toolshed and some shrubs in the back garden, reach the house unseen by the neighbours.

It was autumn then and by the time Jackson reached Wahroonga the light was fading. One day he had just slipped through the fence when he saw Zoe standing motionless behind the toolshed, watching something on the ground. She put her hands to her lips in a gesture asking for silence and pointed. A superb blue-tongued lizard, a good four feet from its nose to the tip of its tail, was moving majestically towards her in its prehistoric waddle, its head and neck moving to the left as it put its front left foot forward. Its body was so low-slung that its leg joints were higher than its backbone and its weird forked tongue flicked continually in and out of its mouth.

'He thinks he's going to get some food,' Zoe said. 'I often throw him a titbit. Isn't he beautiful?'

He was indeed. His slithering bulky body was contained in a wonderful supple dull black skin decorated with bands and dots of grey markings running not only around his belly but down his legs to the long, delicate toes.

'Oh, look!' Zoe exclaimed. 'Here's another.'

A smaller lizard had emerged from the bushes and was stepping slowly towards them. 'I never saw this one before.'

Jackson looked at it carefully.

'It must be a female.'

'Why do you say that?'

'It's smaller and its skin is not so strikingly marked.'

Zoe bent over beside him to look more closely and Jackson noticed how her big breasts seem to swing forward, apparently unconfined by any brassiere, inside her knitted woollen dress.

The male lizard wheeled slowly around and began to follow the female. They both moved in slow motion but the male moved a little faster and soon he was lying immediately behind the female.

'George —,' Zoe whispered, 'you don't think they're going to do anything, do you?'

'I don't know,' Jackson said. Ridiculously, he could feel the blood beginning to pound in his ears.

The female stopped moving and the male strode forward until her passive body lay beneath his.

'My God,' said Zoe. 'They *are* going to. But how do they do it?'

'The way all animals do it, I suppose.' Jackson said.

'But her tail is in the way.'

As though in answer, the female lizard moved her tail to one side. Zoe stepped in front of Jackson to watch more closely. The male lizard seemed to lie on his side and apparently slid his penis beneath the female's tail.

'He's gone in!' Zoe said. 'Look, look!'

She shot out an arm behind her to grip Jackson's leg and as soon as she felt his calf she ran her hand up between his legs. She grabbed him as the male lizard made a series of unmistakable thrusting movements. In a strangled cry, Zoe said. 'Quickly, darling, quickly! Do it now while we're watching them!'

She fell to her knees in front of Jackson and with one hand dragged up her dress behind her. She was wearing nothing beneath it, as was usual on the evenings Jackson visited her; he saw the smooth olive globes of her buttocks and between them her swollen lips, ready for him. Still staring at the lizards, Zoe panted, 'Now, darling! For God's sake, do it now! Can't you see them!'

Jackson, uncontrollably excited, tore at the belt of his slacks and fell upon her from behind. Not taking her eyes off the lizards, Zoe pushed back against him; as he penetrated her she gave a wrenching groan of pleasure.

Afterwards Jackson fell over and lay stunned in the leaves. Zoe knelt beside him, gently stroking his forehead. Her angular face had softened a little, as it did after love making. Immediately before it she often looked strained, almost haggard, but after it her face smoothed out. Jackson glanced at her hair, nearly black, with little kinks in it; she had already tied it back with the ribbon which had come loose in her passion.

'Wasn't that marvellous?' she asked.

Jackson self-consciously scrambled to his feet.

'Suppose a neighbour saw us?'

'The shed and the bushes hide us,' Zoe said. 'The neighbours can't see anything.'

'There was plenty to see,' Jackson muttered, confused and embarrassed.

'It was certainly a bit sudden,' Zoe said, hooking her arm companionably through his. 'But those weird prehistoric things excited me so much I couldn't help myself. It was a moment we just had to seize. I mean, you and I may never see lizards mating again and to make love while we watched them doing it — God! It will never happen to either of us again as long as we live.'

Jackson tucked in his shirt and did up his belt.

'You're shocked, aren't you?' Zoe said.

'Well —'

'Life is for living, Georgie. And anyway, if anybody were to be told that you and I ... well, nobody would believe it. Come on; let's go up to the house and have a drink.'

Jackson threw back his mosquito net and pulled on his perpetually sweat-dampened shirt. He could smell his own feet.

'You awake, George?' Jefferson called quietly from the shallow, square trench of the command post.

'I can't sleep in this heat,' Jackson said.

'Captain Reid phoned from the OP half an hour ago,' Jefferson said. 'Nothing urgent but he asked you to call him when you woke up.'

'Oh, Jesus!' Jackson thought. 'I've got to live with her husband every day now.' He pulled on his trousers and his boots and buckled his anklets web and stumbled over to the field telephone in the command post.

7

The campaign on Saruna lasted eight weeks, during which neither side received any substantial reinforcements. The Japanese tried a couple of times to land more troops but the American planes spotted the little convoys early and mauled them so severely the ships turned back. On the other hand, the Japanese Navy still commanded the sea in the area and the Allied high command apparently took the view that as long as the Australians and Americans were holding out there was no point in risking scarce shipping by trying to send reinforcements by sea. The trickle of men and substantial quantities of ammunition which arrived came by air.

Jackson could not later recall chronologically what happened when during those eight weeks; the campaign became a jumbled memory of discomfort, fear, confusion and above all weariness. The guns seemed always to have to be moved in the mud from one position to another a few hundred yards away and Jackson seemed always to be standing in the rain shouting fire orders to the bedraggled gunners or, crouched, his clothes reeking with sweat, in some slit trench in a clearing with some officer from the infantry which the troop was supporting at the time. Sometimes Jackson thought sardonically of the role of artillery envisaged in the training manuals: an officer respectfully flanked by a signaller and a bombardier perched in some presumably dry and safe nook on the top of a hill peering through binoculars at fully visible enemy targets a mile away, on which he brought down fire from guns snugly dug into gunpits, covered with elaborate camouflage nets, sited behind a hill two or three miles back. The latest supplement to the gunnery manual, which had arrived just before the battery had left Broome, had certainly caught up with the efficient new techniques devised for engaging targets in the Western Desert, but they were of no great assistance for using the 25-pounders on a tropical island covered with copra plantations.

Jackson longingly recalled the exercises carried out at his officers' training school, where everybody travelled in an appointed vehicle labelled in big white letters on the doors to take part in a rite known as the occupation of a position. On Saruna most of 82 Battery's vehicles were useless, either because they stuck in the mud or because there were no roads on which to use them. Moving the guns became a marathon of physical effort in which everybody heaved and pushed and cursed as the old Marmons bucked and skidded like fractious elephants. After the first week of the campaign everybody in the battery was issued with a pair of gumboots which had apparently been hoarded God knows where in some quartermaster's store; Jackson, so busy that he flopped down to get a little sleep whenever he could, once did not take his gumboots off for five days; he was horrified when he saw the wrinkled, spongy mass of flesh which used to be his feet. At night, Shannahan spoke to him several times, and once Zoe Reid whispered in his ear, 'Oh God, you're big.'

That happened when Jackson was dozing, his nerves taut, in a corner of a slit trench in a laager, the name given to a system used by the infantry to guard against infiltration by the Japanese at night. A platoon would protect itself by moving in the afternoon to some area clear of trees, where the men would dig as many slit trenches as necessary, all close together. If possible, they also surrounded the laager with trip wires from which hung empty ration tins with pebbles or rifle bullets inside them to rattle if somebody touched the trip wire. At nightfall everybody got into a trench and stayed there until dawn, whether their bowels moved or not. If any shape was seen moving about in the blackness it was assumed to be Japanese.

Sometimes Japanese hidden in the plantation nearby would try to provoke the men in the laager to open fire and thus reveal their exact position. Jackson several times heard voices calling, in oddly accented English, 'Hey, you Aussie, we fuck your wife soon,' or 'Hey, you man from Briserbane (or Shydernee) we fuck your sister — how you like that?' Sometimes the Japanese used common women's Christian names. One night a Japanese who seemed to be only feet away called out, 'Hey, we be in Osteralie soon. We make Mary eat Japanese cock.' The hulking Company Sergeant Major with whom Jackson was sharing a trench whispered in his ear, 'Bloody Nip will be lucky. I can't get her to put her hand on mine.'

Jackson came to realise what formidable troops well-trained Australians were — physically tough, very practical, careful about essentials, careless of military frippery, very brave in their slouching, cigarette-smoking way and ruthless when necessary. One night out of a profound silence around a laager there suddenly came the grunting and thudding sounds of men in hand to hand combat. A Japanese marine crawling into the laager had been seized by a couple of Australians, one of whom held him in a bear-like grip while the other killed him by driving a jungle knife into his chest. Not a word of Japanese or English was spoken.

In the daytime there were several charges by groups of marines, all beaten back by steady and accurate Australian small arms fire. Many times concentrations from 82 Battery and the infantry's three-inch mortars landing on likely forming-up areas out of sight in the jungle probably broke up other attacks. Australian patrols, pushing forward, were under orders to take at least a few prisoners for interrogation. Brigade HQ was given a couple of privates from a labour company which had been put ashore with the Japanese marines, but it never got a living marine.

The shaven-headed marines wore strange pudding-basin helmets, painted green, and bifurcated sandshoes, with four toes in one pocket and the big toe in a separate compartment, apparently designed to allow them to climb trees easily. Their tactics puzzled the Australians. Marines would climb coconut trees, tie themselves into the cluster of branches at the top and then fire on Australian patrols passing beneath them. They were poor shots and usually missed hitting anybody in the patrol, but they were invariably shot dead in their tree. Sometimes the marine would have roped his body to the trunk and did not fall down, no matter how often he was hit. Sometimes, having roped his feet to the tree, he would fall, jerk to the end of his rope and swing by his feet in a ghastly upside-down parody of hanging.

After three weeks the Japanese assault had been halted well short of the airstrip and the Australians gradually began to push the attackers back towards the north of the island, but the price in casualties from gunshot wounds and malaria or dengue fever had been heavy and the troops were dog-tired. The battery's anachronistically named Wagon Lines Officer, a red-headed insurance salesman aged twenty-three, was killed with two men when the Japanese rushed an old hut being used as a forward ammunition dump. A gunlayer broke his leg when the spade of his gun dropped on it as it was being unhooked from the tractor. A man in K Troop died of a violent attack of food poisoning. Three men in J Troop were wounded by shells fired from a strange little man-pulled gun with solid wheels which the Japanese had brought ashore. But one event particularly depressed 82 Battery. Two of the signallers sitting patiently at a maintenance terminal by the phone line linking the two troops were ambushed by a Japanese patrol, tied to trees and bayoneted to death.

By the fifth week the guns were down to crews of three, a Number 1, a layer and a loading number. Men who had malaria now refused to report sick, but carried on as best they could, enduring the shaking and twisting and teeth-chattering in the periods of rigour, and staggering, hollow-eyed and tremble-handed, about their tasks between attacks. Some were so weak they could not lift a 25-pounder shell without pausing for breath. Jackson had a sharp attack of diarrhoea and felt ashamed of the smell of shit which seemed to cling to his body. Reid religiously shaved every day, if necessary in cold water, but he was becoming thinner and his nose beakier.

The infantry were doggedly sending out patrols, which

reported the Japanese were steadily being pushed back. But it was clear the Australians would not be physically capable of continuing indefinitely. It was at this point that the American planes spotted a convoy of Japanese ships heading for Saruna. When this news circulated among the troops, a great wave of despair swept over them. They realised that strong reinforcements for the Japanese marines would be the deciding factor and the Saruna defending force would be overrun. Many men scribbled a last note to a wife, mother or girl friend and gave it to a mate in the hope he would survive to deliver it. A Catholic padre attached to the brigade came up to an ancient water tank near one of the plantation tracks and heard confessions and gave absolution to those troops who could be spared to reach him. In 82 Battery a silence seemed to fall over the gunners at the thought of what might lie ahead for them. A lance bombardier gave Jackson a ring to give to his mother, if possible. A driver tore up the picture of a plump pretty girl he had carried in his wallet for three years. 'Don't want the bastards even to look at her,' he said. 'Not those bastards.'

News of the Japanese convoy kept passing down to the troops from the American Air Force via Brigade. The Americans did not manage to break up the convoy, now reported to include a couple of destroyers and a troop-landing ship. One afternoon the news filtered through from the battery command post to the J Troop command post that the Japanese ships had been sighted very close to the northern tip of Saruna when night fell. Next morning the ships were well clear of the island but the Kittyhawk pilots reported foot and vehicle tracks running across the sand where the landing barges had touched the beach. The US planes strafed the Japanese ships all the next day and the ships all fought back fiercely, but did not flee away to safety northwards, so the brigadier commanding Saruna deduced correctly that the troop carrier was preparing to put another wave of barges ashore during the next night. Next morning there were more tracks across the sand but these were on the opposite side of the island's narrow tip. The Japanese ships were scuttling away north at full speed. The brigadier could do nothing but spread the forces he had left to cover the plantation roads.

J Troop was still supporting the AIF infantry battalion and Jefferson, who had been FOO for forty-eight hours, had been warned that Captain Reid would relieve him at 1000 hours. Reid, having slept as best he could at the gun position, was checking all the still-pertinent registered targets on the GPO's artillery board when the phone from the battery command post buzzed. The bombardier answered the phone and passed the handset to Reid. Jackson, feeling and looking filthy, was shaving in cold water. He heard Reid, at the phone, suddenly shout, 'Good Christ!' and saw him throw the phone back on its cradle. Dulled by tiredness, Jackson stood razor in hand, wondering what grim news had come down the phone. Sergeant Major Docker, who had of course already shaved, came loping up, indicating by his frown that officers were not supposed to behave like that. Reid shouted to him, 'Leave one man on each gun and get everybody else here at once.'

'Everybody?' said Docker. 'Wouldn't it be better —'

'Do what you're fucking told,' Reid snapped.

Docker, full of prim indignation, turned away and began to gather up the men. When everybody was assembled Reid said, 'Be ready to take post if we get fire orders, but I wanted to tell you something important. The infantry has had patrols out all night and they have discovered that the Japanese convoy we all know about did not come bringing reinforcements; it came to take the Japanese off. Every bastard has gone — all the living ones. The Nips must have given up hope of taking the strip and they have pulled out.'

There was a long silence while the gunners' weary minds struggled with the news and then Lance Bombardier Satherley, a cheerful roughneck with a paybook full of red ink, suddenly shouted, 'Jesus, what a bit of news!' He threw his arms around Reid and hugged him. 'You fucking beauty!' he shouted.

Half a dozen men, laughing and talking at once, crowded

around Reid as though he had personally been responsible for their deliverance. Reid laughed happily with them; Jackson had never seen him so close to the men.

It took only a week or ten days to mop up the few Japanese who had missed being picked up off the beaches. As the Australian infantry moved steadily forward right to the top of the island they came across the detritus of a defeated enemy — field kitchens, piles of unused medical stores, a surprising quantity of french letters (although the only women on Saruna were the few islanders still living in their officially abandoned village at the far southern end), piles of undestroyed orders and unit nominal rolls and, of course, bodies. Although the infantry had strict orders to take some prisoners, they reported that they did not reach anybody alive. In several cases, a soldier lying on the ground near death from an old wound had kept one hand grenade. If he had the strength, he tried to throw it at the approaching Australians. If he was too weak, he held the grenade against his own chest and pulled the pin. In one case, he took with him an Australian soldier who was bending over him. As many an Australian soldier said in tones of puzzled respect, 'These bastards don't care if they die or not.'

J Troop engaged its last target of the campaign as a sort of ballistic picnic. The infantry had reported that a few Japanese might still be sheltering on a minuscule vine-covered sand spit, measuring about fifty yards across, lying a few hundred yards off the northern tip of the island. J Troop was assigned to work it over. The rain had ceased, the tractors bowled noisily up the dirt road towing the guns, turned off into a big clearing and did an almost normal occupation. The OP was established in comfort behind a bush near the beach. Bombardier Richards was allowed to do the shoot with Reid acting as his assistant and Jackson as a critic. At the guns, the four sergeants took turns as GPO. Richards shot well and the sergeants made a fair hash of things, but finally the little sand patch, which was later found to contain no Japanese anyway, was scarified. Eventually Reid called 'Cease fire', put his binoculars back in their case, sighed and said, 'Well, that's the end of the action on Saruna.'

'And thank God,' said Jackson.

'Perhaps,' Reid said. 'Perhaps. You know what the man said — war consists of long periods of boredom punctuated by short periods of fright. I hope the first doesn't turn out to be worse than the second.'

When they arrived back at the gun position a long message was waiting for Reid. It outlined Brigade instructions that henceforth Atebrin was to be swallowed by the troops at a daily parade supervised by an officer, who was to observe personally that the tablets went down.

Reid showed the message to Jackson.

'See what I mean?' he said.

8

As he recovered from his exhaustion in the weeks immediately after the cease-fire, Jackson found that he not only thought about Zoe a lot but he was filled once again by a leaden sensation of guilt and betrayal, made worse now by the daily, usually hourly, presence of her husband.

It was Reid himself who had introduced Zoe to Jackson. The regiment had been one of the Australian units involved in the first true rupture of the umbilical cord between Mother England and dutiful daughter Australia. When the Japanese began their relentless march southwards after the fall of Singapore, the Australian Labor government led by John Curtin decided that Australian troops were needed to defend Australia and defied Churchill's demand that those in North Africa and the Middle East be left there to advance the campaign against Italy and Germany.

The Australian units were rushed home, intended to land in Indonesia, perhaps, to make a stand there, but the Japanese moved south so fast that there was soon nowhere for the Australians to go except Australia. Thus the regiment was disembarked in Melbourne and sent by a four-day train journey to the hutted camp at Cowra in New South Wales, from which, after ten days, the men were sent on one week's leave, presumably to give the high command more time to think what to do. Jackson joined the regiment on its second day in Cowra, but he was nevertheless sent on leave with everybody else; he knew by now not to waste time trying to fathom the inscrutable workings of the army. The train taking them to Sydney, dragged along by a venerable P-class loco leaking steam at every joint, jolted slowly along with many stops. Sometimes the officers got out of their carriage and strolled down the platform to chat to the men, exchanging cigarettes and little insiders' jokes. Jackson, feeling unbearably unblooded and unnecessary, kept to himself, feeling his face burning with embarrassment. Reid must have noticed this, for when the train chugged out of Bathurst he sat down beside Jackson and made conversation.

'None of us have had a chance to talk to you much,' he said pleasantly. 'I won't have much chance either — I've been warned I'm to go to bloody Divvy staff soon and become a trained seal.'

The news did not surprise Jackson who, not having met any, imagined that divisional staff officers were a breed of mentally superior planners. Reid, he knew, was regarded as the Einstein of the regiment because of his arcane job in civil life; he was a university lecturer in pure mathematics. His nickname was unusual, too. It was 'Tut'. Jackson had only recently heard the celebrated story of its creation.

It seemed that one Sunday, in the unit's first camp in Australia, some gunners were sitting in their eight-holer latrine, having a companionable crap in the morning sunlight, when Gunner Malloy, R. J., who had been turning the pages of an old copy of the *National Geographic* magazine, suddenly shouted, 'Shit!'

According to one version, a mate asked, 'Is that an order?' According to another version a lance bombardier said, 'Quit skiting. I beat you to it a minute ago.' But at all events Malloy held up the *National Geographic* and said, 'Look at this. It's Reidy!'

He was pointing to an article about the discovery of the tomb of Tutankhamen illustrated with a full-page picture of the pharaoh's golden death mask. True enough, something about the super-smooth skin, the high forehead and the self-confident repose of the face irresistibly suggested Christopher Reid who was, from that moment nicknamed Tutankhamen, soon shortened to Tut. Glancing at the man sitting beside him in the train, with the Africa Star and a little bit of metal meaning Mentioned in Dispatches on the chest of a uniform made to measure in expensive barathea, Jackson felt over-awed. He mumbled something obvious about the slowness of the train.

'I remember the first time the regiment went into camp,' Reid said. 'My god — what a circus! When we took the train from Central to Ingleburn, half the men were drunk and they kept screaming "Chocco!" at the sight of some poor bloody call-up. Six or seven of our blokes arrived riding on the roof of one of the carriages, two of them tried to get into the cab and drive the engine and somebody fell out a window and landed in hospital. We were all being great big AIF diggers.'

'Everybody is much quieter now,' Jackson said.

'Oh yes,' said Reid. 'Discipline is replacing *Smith's Weekly* at last. We are coming to realise that armies work better if people just do what they're told. And of course we've been overseas and seen some other armies.' He laughed. 'That's a great awakener. Before we went to the Middle East I somehow imagined that I was a sunburnt Aussie and taller and bigger than the weedy Poms. I got a shock when I went on leave in Cairo and found myself continually passing soldiers from British regiments who were bigger than I was. Well, let's see if we can get a bit of a snooze before the maelstrom on Central Station.'

It was certainly not a quiet arrival. When the train finally limped into Sydney's Central Station, the gunners, with leave passes already in their pockets, poured whooping and yelling off the train into the sepulchral chamber of the assembly platform to join the waiting crowd of wives, children, sisters, mothers, girl friends and even a few pet dogs. Reid was met by a dark girl in a long loose coat. She did not throw her arms around Reid's neck and kiss him, laughing or crying, as most of the women did; she put one arm around his waist and hugged him affectionately. Reid, looking as self-possessed as ever, kissed her on the cheek as though he had only been away for a day. Jackson was about to slip past them when Reid said, 'Oh, George — this is my wife Zoe.'

Jackson shook hands with Reid's wife. She had strong

hands and her nearly black hair was so crinkly it seemed like wire. Her expression was serious, almost sombre, but beneath the heavy arched eyebrows she had eyes of a striking violet colour. She and Jackson exchanged no more than a few banalities before she and Reid strolled away, chatting.

Jackson did not enjoy the start of his leave much.

His university friends had either enlisted or been called up or were immersed in a civilian life which now seemed to Jackson to be remote and dreary; the girl with whom he had been going about when he enlisted, a nurse, had herself joined up and was in the Air Force in Darwin. Consequently Jackson was surprised and delighted to get a phone call from Reid on the second last day of the leave, asking him to come to what Reid called 'a bit of a booze-up at our place in Wahroonga'.

The 'place in Wahroonga' turned out to be a delightful, creaking, shabby Federation house with wonderful wide verandahs and the original coloured glass in the front door which opened into a long straight hall running right down the centre of the building. The house was set in a big unkempt garden in which giant hibiscus bushes seemed to be running wild.

There were about twenty people standing or sitting on the verandah. A couple were officers from the regiment. A couple more were other ranks — Reid's bombardier assistant and a driver who had been one of his students at the university among them. There were two young Air Force officers, a sailor in square rig, a brigadier, and a few civilians, including three or four grey-haired men. The women were assorted grandmothers, mothers, wives and pig-tailed young sisters. Most people were drinking home-brewed beer made by Reid's father, the jovial manager of a big insurance company, who seemed to have brought along several dozen bottles with corks held down by string looped around the bottle's neck. Reid, immaculate but looking strange in a pair of grey flannel trousers and an old blazer with some sort of pocket on it, circulated urbanely filling glasses and pointing out that there was a good reason for keeping them full. The brew tasted quite like a well-known, and then quite unobtainable, South Australian brand; each bottle had a little layer of sediment on the bottom. If somebody poured only one glass and set the bottle upright again, the sediment diffused through the remaining beer and spoilt it; the trick was to keep pouring, once a bottle was opened, in one smooth movement until the bottle was empty. As a result of this technical requirement, everybody's glass was continually in the process of being topped up, the men, including Jackson, became flushed, the women grew giggly and the noise of the conversation became deafening.

Jackson was at home with people like these, but he no longer felt one of them; it even felt strange to be going out in public in a civilian's shirt and slacks. He wondered at the lack of curiosity about the war; intelligent people followed it closely on the radio and in the newspapers but nobody seemed to ask servicemen more than a few perfunctory questions about what they had done. Having listened while a schoolgirl prattled on about her homework, Jackson was standing talking in a group of men when Zoe Reid came up and said, 'Come on now, you mob; spread your charms among the ladies.' As the men rather sheepishly moved away, Zoe put her hand on Jackson's arm and said, 'And you come and talk to me.'

Sitting him on a tatty old sofa on the verandah, she said, 'I know most of the officers in the unit but I don't think we've met before. Did you transfer from another regiment?'

'No, I'm a reinforcement officer,' Jackson muttered.

'Well, don't look so hang-dog about it.'

Zoe was looking at him intently.

'Did I sound hang-dog?'

'Of course you did. That's silly.'

'I feel a fraud. Everybody around here has been in action except me.'

'When did you enlist?' Zoe asked.

'May 1940,' Jackson said.

'Well, you enlisted before some of the men in the regiment — if that's important.'

'I expect I would have been overseas already if I hadn't been grabbed for officers' training,' said Jackson.

'I'd be very surprised if the men in the regiment hold anything against you. You may get some resentment from a few of the sergeants or warrant officers, but that's all.'

'The colonel thinks I'm a useless appendage.'

'Old Jack thinks his wife is a useless appendage,' Zoe said. 'But she keeps him right in his place. The fact is there will be enough war to go around. You may see more of it than you want before it's over.'

What a strange conversation to have with a woman, Jackson thought; obviously she understands a good deal about army life.

Somebody in the garden called out to her then and she called back, 'Coming, coming'. As she stood up Jackson felt the tips of her fingers slide slowly across the knuckles of his hand on the back of the sofa. He looked at Zoe quickly; she was looking away from him into the garden. Turning towards him, she said, 'I'm glad you could come; I hope we'll see you again sometime.'

Driving home in his old jalopy Jackson argued furiously with himself — did she touch me on purpose? Or did her hand just slip off the back of the sofa by accident? He stopped his car and, placing his hand on the back of the front seat, tried to work out how it could have been an accident. Finally he drove home feeling disturbed.

9

Jackson's father was a doctor with a well-established general practice conducted from his big house in Turramurra, all little gables and turrets, in a street lined with camphor laurel trees so big they met in an arch above the roadway. Dr Jackson practised in the halcyon days when even a GP was a god and patients might not even be told what was wrong with them. ('We'll get you into hospital, Mrs Hetherington, and fix up that little trouble in your tummy.') Dr Jackson had been a young army doctor in Flanders in World War I. Having survived a conflict in which Australia, with a population of five million, had produced 417 000 servicemen and women, every one a volunteer, and suffered 226 000 dead and wounded, he was unimpressed by the casualty rate of his son's war. Jackson's mother seemed to regard World War II merely as a nuisance to be coped with, like a train drivers' strike. She was also largely occupied in putting a brave face on a family scandal which had sent frissons through every tennis party in Turramurra; one of Jackson's middle-aged uncles was openly living with a woman to whom he was not married. One way and another, Jackson found that he had become a sort of visitor, welcome, but still transient, in his own home. He began to wish he was back in the unit.

On the day before his leave was up, the phone rang and his mother said. 'It's for you, dear — I think it's the Army.'

'Is that you, George?' said a voice, far away in the crackling. 'Hamilton here.'

Hamilton was the adjutant of the regiment who, with the CO and the captain quartermaster, had somewhat mysteriously remained in Cowra.

'I'm calling you to let you know orders have come in about your movements,' Hamilton said, 'and I wanted to make sure you got word before you left Sydney. In fact, George, don't leave Sydney. You are to go to a three-week Eastern Command bridge-building course at the Engineers' Depot in Moore Park. You have to report on Monday.'

'Am I being transferred?' Jackson asked, confused.

'No, no!' the adjutant said. 'You're being sent to learn all about building bridges at a moment's notice over a creek or ravine or whatnot so we can take the guns across if we lose our road map.'

'But, for God's sake! I've only just joined the unit. I mean, wouldn't some other officer —'

'Ours is not to reason why,' said Hamilton, who had acquired the essential adjutant's knack of passing on orders without giving the slightest indication whether he approved of them or not. In fact, Hamilton was fully aware that the CO had already been briefed for an imminent move out of Australia again and, regarding the bridge-building course as a piece of lunacy dreamed up by Division, had nominated the officer who, in his view, could most easily be spared from the urgent work of preparing the unit for jungle warfare. This officer was of course the greenhorn Jackson.

What Hamilton said to Jackson was simply, 'You all clear, George? Report to the Engineers' Depot at 0900 next Monday. I'm sending you a written signal to confirm all this, of course.'

When Jackson hung up his mother said, 'What's the matter, dear? Not bad news, I hope?'

'I don't know,' Jackson said. 'Apparently I'm to go to a school in Sydney for three weeks.'

'You mean you'll be here for another three weeks!' said his mother. 'Oh, Georgie! That's wonderful. What a shame Barbara's in Darwin!'

'Yes, it is a bit of a pity,' Jackson muttered. He put on an old sweater and went out for a walk, trying not to think of Zoe Reid.

It had taken him a long time to persuade his nurse to go

beyond allowing his hand to explore her and to take off her all-cotton pants so they could make love — in the back of his car, inevitably. They both dutifully read van der Velde, the manual of the day, and had worked their way through about half the positions, with much careful post-coitum inspection of french letters, by the time Jackson enlisted. The nurse was a happy, well-scrubbed girl who, with vague thoughts of marriage, made love in a well-scrubbed sort of way, but she had never, Jackson admitted guiltily to himself, thrilled him as much as Zoe Reid had merely by touching his hand. He had been dutifully writing to his nurse but, recalling his last letter to her and re-reading her last letter to him, thought with irritation that they might be brother and sister.

He found the bridge-building school uninspiring, too. It was largely concerned with lashing tree-trunks together in complicated ways to form trestles and putting down other trunks to form a roadway. The trunks, pre-cut and much used in previous schools, were stacked at the depot. Although the instructors remarked that later the school would move out into some bush for a day or two to cut down some real trees and make a bridge over a real creek, the idea seemed to fill them with foreboding. The students were warrant officers and lieutenants from various arms, including the RAE itself, the infantry, the signals corps and the RAASC. The daily trip from his home to the depot and back seemed to Jackson to symbolise only too clearly how little a genuine soldier he had become; he was merely a day boy, ashamed to be sitting beside men who wore the Africa Star. He was thoroughly depressed when Zoe Reid rang him up.

On the telephone she sounded unexpectedly girlish and brisk; she might have been an Abbotsleigh prefect. Reid had trouble reconciling this voice with the brooding, almost sad, face.

'Chris tells me you've drawn the bridge-building course,' Zoe said. 'Lucky devil.'

'Is he in Sydney?' Jackson asked, off-balance.

'Oh, no. He's gone back to the unit to pack up his gear

and move to the gilded staff. I understand the bridge thing is for subalterns, anyway — the adjutants probably put the names into a hat.'

'Sounds like the Army,' Jackson agreed.

'Bill Tildsley from 2/43 has been sent to do the course. He and his wife are old mates of ours and they're coming round with a few other people for a rough old lunch on Saturday. It would be nice if you could come, too.'

'Well, I —' Jackson stammered.

There was no reason why he should not accept a quite normal invitation to a routine suburban gathering. He would be at home with the people there, yet his body, less confused than his mind, sent him a warning signal and he hesitated.

'Do come,' said Zoe, 'I'm sure you'll enjoy yourself.'

Jackson accepted. All that evening he tormented himself trying to deduce if her last remark had any hidden meaning and vowing that when he went to the Reids' house again he would keep as far away from Zoe as politeness would allow.

On Saturday he found seven or eight people chatting around a table in the shade of a big scribbly gum. Zoe greeted him with off-hand friendliness and he attached himself to a big bespectacled young housewife with a baby in a high-wheeled Kensington-style pram beside her. She spoke at some length on the difficulty of getting butter. Zoe's father was not there this time, but he was represented by what seemed like gallons of his home-brewed beer and Jackson drank more than he intended. Secretly glancing at Zoe, he noticed again how crinkly her hair was; she had pulled the thick mop back and tied it with a dark red ribbon behind her head. She wore a simple, belted cotton dress beneath which, Jackson's instinctive male X-ray deduced, was a body which could not be far short of voluptuous. Her frame was so wiry that Jackson could clearly see the collar-bones and even the start of the sternum, but below that two heavy breasts swelled out on top of a small waist and below that again Zoe had a big bottom which curved in suddenly on top of athletic legs with big calf muscles; the swellings and diminishings of her body reminded Jackson of pen and ink sketches by some of the old masters.

When Jackson went to the house to get a cigarette-puffing old hospital matron an ashtray, he found Zoe washing up in the kitchen sink and chatting to a jovial grandmother and a sunburned young naval able seaman. Seeing Jackson, she smiled over her shoulder and the male radar which young men involuntarily bounce off women they meet, and which correctly or incorrectly brings back the answer 'available' or 'not available', scanned Zoe and flashed up 'available'.

Flustered, Jackson grabbed an ashtray and was half out the door when Zoe asked him, 'How's the bridge building?

'OK,' said Jackson. 'I've learned how to lash logs together, anyway.'

'Isn't Chris being transferred somewhere?' asked the grandmother. 'Goodness, the Army can't leave anybody in one place, can they?'

'I've just had a letter from Cowra,' Zoe said, wiping a plate. 'He's to join Division in Brisbane on the eighteenth.' She glanced at the wall calendar. 'That's, let me see ... thirteen days from now.' She hung up the teatowel. 'Chris will have left the regiment before you get back, George. I hope you said a good-bye to him.'

Was this, Jackson wondered, some sort of message? If so, he could not decode it. Floundering, he hurried back to the garden. His heart, he realised, was beating so strongly he could feel the thump in his ears.

'Don't you think so, Mr Jackson?' somebody's aunt was asking.

'Think about what?' Jackson asked.

'I knew you weren't listening,' she said. 'I was saying what a shame it is that our lovely Australian bush is full of all sorts of awful creatures — lizards and goannas and things. Poor Zoe has a huge lizard of some sort that lives in the garden here; she seems quite fond of it.'

'Make a nice handbag,' grunted a cadaverous flight lieutenant.

Zoe came out on the verandah and clapped her hands.

'Grub's ready,' she said. 'It's stew today, just to make all you military types feel at home. George, how about you and Ted help carry out a few things?'

Jackson and the flight lieutenant went into the kitchen where Zoe was giving out trays of food. With perfect naturalness she kept George's tray until after the other people had left the kitchen. She faced George and without coquetry slid one hand behind his head and kissed him. When he felt the warm cushion of her lips, George half made to pull back. Zoe looked at him almost mockingly and kissed him again, this time with the warm tip of her tongue, and gripped suddenly by desire he seized her in his arms and thrust his own tongue between her lips. Zoe gave a small strangled moan and sucked his tongue into her mouth so hard it felt as though she was trying to pull it out. Through the hand he had behind her back he felt her muscles tense as she jammed the cheeks of her buttocks together. She pressed her stomach violently against his and he felt the hard bump of her mons veneris. Zoe strained fiercely for perhaps ten seconds and then gave a long breath out and fell back.

'Oh, Christ,' she said. 'I didn't expect to do that.'

'You mean —' Jackson stammered. 'Have you —'

'Of course I have,' she said. 'You . . . affect me. Or haven't you noticed?'

She looked suddenly haggard.

Jackson was nonplussed. It would have been correct, he felt, if she had cried, or said something about 'Oh, God, how did this happen,' or even brazened it out. But Zoe merely turned away and leaned back against the sink and said, 'Don't worry, I'm not a talker and I hope you're not.'

'No, of course not,' Jackson mumbled.

'Well, take that bloody tray out to the people, will you? And, if you feel like it, you could ring me up.'

10

Jackson rang up.

For the rest of the bridge-building course he lived through a sexual adventure beyond any of his feverish schoolday fantasies. Sometimes, when bridge building finished early he would drive straight to Wahroonga and, parking his battered old Overland well away, would walk up to Zoe's house through the bush behind it. Sometimes on vague and increasingly strange excuses he would leave his parents' home after dinner and go to Zoe until after midnight. Jackson knew he was building up a tremendous reservoir of guilt but he put the future out of his mind in the delirium of the moment. He had never imagined that a 'nice' woman would make love with such relentless determination and concupiscent ingenuity as Zoe Reid.

It was always Zoe who decided when and in which manner they would make love. Jackson, the pupil, learned never to be surprised. Once Zoe said to him, 'A lot of people despise the old knee trembler, but don't you worry — it can be good fun. Here, I'll show you.' She took him out to the verandah steps at the back of the house where, standing one step higher than Jackson, she pulled up her dress. 'The woman must be higher than the man. It puts pressure on a good place and — oh!' Zoe always seemed capable of reaching three or four climaxes and she was delighted when Jackson discovered to his overt astonishment and secret pride that he could repeat the act of love ten or fifteen minutes after the first time.

When Jackson's nurse reached orgasm she would sigh deeply and say a few moments later, 'Oh, darling, that was lovely.' When Zoe reached the first of her orgasms she could give a terrible, wrenching groan as though she had been pierced not by flesh but by red-hot steel and at the end of the series would fall back as though she had been stunned with a club. Once or twice Jackson thought she had lost consciousness but she opened her superb violet eyes a few seconds later and gulped in air with a convulsion which shook her whole body.

Jackson came to realise that he was not the first man with whom Zoe had been unfaithful to Reid. In fact, he once asked her directly and she answered equally directly, 'No, darling, you're not but . . .' — her eyes travelled fondly, almost maternally, over his face from his hair to his chin and she took his hand and kissed the back of it gently — 'you're the sweetest, though.' She had never said, or hinted, that she loved Jackson and she never tried to inveigle him into saying he loved her. Jackson's feelings were inextricably confused; he enjoyed her company and admired her knowledge, far greater than his, of what was going on in the world. Sometimes, seeing her in the grip of her own desire, teeth clenched, face gaunt, striving for one more orgasm, he felt a great pity for her and, on its heels, a great affection. But love — what was that? It could not be the fever generated in the clandestine hothouse of Zoe's body. On the other hand, it had to be more than the comradely feelings he had towards his nurse, of whom, he realised guiltily, he now hardly thought.

Love, Jackson reasoned to himself, was surely an emotion which one person felt towards another to the exclusion at that level of all other persons. The ease with which Zoe had accommodated more than one man in her life shocked Jackson. It even made him uneasy when Zoe, often lying in his arms with the sweat drying on her breasts, spoke casually of small mundane moments of her life with Chris. Once Jackson sat up abruptly and said, 'My God, Zoe, we're really a pair of shits! About Chris, I mean. God, this is his bed and I've stolen his wife . . .'

'You haven't stolen his wife at all,' Zoe interrupted. 'I

am and will remain Chris's wife and with a bit of luck we could have a happy and prosperous life together. I don't feel like having children just yet, but I expect I will.'

'But you can't love Chris if you go on like this.'

'I don't know if I love him, as you call it, or not, but we have known each other since our schooldays, we have a lot of common interests, I have enough education to understand what he is saying, he is amusing and considerate and I admire him — that can't be a bad basis for a marriage, surely.'

Jackson groped with this view of roses around the cottage door.

'But how can you justify us?'

'I don't try,' said Zoe.

They were lying squeezed together into the big armchair on the arm of which she had just ridden him like a jockey. As he struggled for an answer, she asked, 'Does Chris strike you as a man with a certain reserve? Good company, but not "hail fellow well met"?'

'That's right,' said Jackson, 'but I hardly know him.'

'Well, Chris lives a tremendous mental life. Did you know he's written a book about the early history of Tasmania? Or that he's a marvellous photographer? Here . . . have you ever seen his darkroom?'

'What darkroom?'

'I'll show you,' Zoe said, jumping up and walking naked down the hall. She opened a door halfway down and Jackson saw a room equipped with what he guessed was a quite professional darkroom, fitted even with a print-glazer. Leaning against the sink, Zoe added, 'He's had prints in a lot of exhibitions. And he rowed for the university, you know. But he's not a sexpot. I mean, he doesn't seem to have his share of libido. After we were married he made a big effort but soon dropped down to making love once a week. Me — you know me. I could have done it three times a day. Whenever I got excited Chris used to do his damnedest to look after me, but he couldn't keep pace no matter what I did.'

Jackson imagined what she would do and he felt a sharp stab of jealousy.

She switched off the darkroom light and led him back to the sitting room.

'This life between you and Chris,' Jackson said cautiously, 'do you think it can go on?'

'Why not?' said Zoe. 'You've no idea how well Chris and I get along together. Sometimes, I wonder if we do get along because Chris is a secret sort of man — you never know how much he knows. I even wonder whether he doesn't know that I've broken out a couple of times and sort of understands it. But he's never said anything.'

'Good God,' Jackson said, truly shocked. 'You mean he's known you've been unfaithful and not done anything?'

'Such as beat me up or start a divorce?' Zoe laughed. 'I can't imagine Chris doing that. And you must remember, Chris has a great number of intellectual interests to fall back on. In fact, I've wondered how he got along in the Army. I expected him to find regimental life very boring.'

'I don't really know him,' Jackson said.

'I just felt from one or two things he said when he was on leave that he was getting a bit of a shut-in feeling.' She shrugged. 'But he'll cope. Men like Chris don't join the Army for a rest or fun.' She turned towards the mirror to tie her hair back again and as she raised her arm, Jackson saw her breasts lift. They were at the very edge of being overblown; they drooped a fraction under their own weight. My God, they're big, Jackson thought, how big? He slid his right hand, palm straight and parallel to the ground, beneath Zoe's right breast and found the nipple within its great dark aureole projected well beyond the edge of his hand. Jackson slowly closed his fingers on the warm melon of flesh. Zoe, with a tremor of pleasure, twisted quickly in his arms. 'Kiss me, kiss me . . . .'

Two days before Jackson was due to return to the unit he arrived at Zoe's house to find her in the sitting room, looking unexpectedly formal in a dress, shoes and stockings. There was an opened telegram turned face downwards on the coffee table. Instead of immediately taking him in her arms as she usually did, she kissed him on the cheek; she looked worried.

'There's something I have to tell you,' she said. 'I am most profoundly sorry about what has happened and I ask you to believe that I had no idea this situation would come about.'

'What situation?' Jackson asked, alarmed.

'I have just heard that Chris is not to be transferred to the staff after all. He is to stay with the regiment. Apparently he only heard about it yesterday and he wired me to tell me to go on writing to the unit. There's his telegram.'

Jackson read it twice.

'Good God!' he said. 'Your husband and I will be in the same unit. We might end up in the same battery.'

'Exactly,' said Zoe.

'Oh, I'll never talk,' Jackson said hastily.

'Oh, don't be stupid!' Zoe burst out. 'I never imagined for a second that you would. It's not that! It's, well ... you're a nice man and you may find it a bit of a strain to have to meet my husband day after day. Oh, bugger everything! I wouldn't have done this in a million years if Chris hadn't been going to leave the unit next month. Darling, I'm so sorry.'

Jackson read the telegram for the third time. 'What does Chris mean when he says "Will be very busy here"?'

'I think he is trying to tell me something is happening in the unit. They're getting ready for something — probably to go overseas again, to New Guinea, I suppose. If that were the case any colonel would put up a fight to keep his most experienced officers with the unit.'

Zoe put the telegram back in its envelope. 'I'll get some tea.'

She went out to the kitchen, came back with a tray and sat down on the other side of the coffee table.

'What's all this about?' Jackson asked. 'You haven't even kissed me properly yet.'

'I feel a bit disturbed by that wire,' said Zoe. 'I have a strong feeling of having done something nasty to you. I'll get some milk.'

Jackson followed her into the kitchen, a big dark room which always smelt faintly of vegetables.

'After all we've done,' he said, 'what difference can it make what we do now? Come here and kiss me.'

'Honestly, George, I'd rather not. Later perhaps, but not just now.'

With a lightning lunge Jackson reached across the kitchen table and grabbed Zoe by the arm. 'We're not going to end all this by sitting around like two Methodists in a church hall,' he said. 'Put down that milk jug and kiss me.'

Trying to pull her arm free, Zoe said angrily, 'I've told you, George, I don't want to.'

'Bugger what you want!' said Jackson, suddenly furious. 'We started making love because you wanted to and we do it the ways you want and the number of times you want. Am I just a child with a big cock? I want you now, this minute. Take your clothes off.'

'Let me go at once!'

George seized the bottom of her dress in his two fists, one beside each knee, and pulled it upwards with such force that it flew up beneath her armpits with the sound of tearing fabric. Zoe, he saw, was wearing a funny baggy pair of white cotton pants. 'Take those off,' he said.

'I won't,' Zoe shouted.

George grabbed the top of the pants with one strong sunburned hand and yanked downwards. The pants shot to the floor leaving Zoe before him in a tableau he never forgot; she was half-crouched like a wrestler, with her arms up defensively in front of her, her hair flying, her eyes wide, not with fear, but with amazement, the white skin stretched drum-taut over the bones of her face. Her torn dress sagged down outside one leg and the great thatch of pubic hair made a dark mysterious forest beneath the absurd frilly straps of a white suspender belt. Beside himself, Jackson threw her to the floor and took her on the cold brown linoleum while one of her feet, entangled with the stool, rattled it ludicrously against the table. Jackson never knew what happened on the floor, but when he had finished and rolled over on his back, he was feeling not elation, but a devastating and bewildering sense of failure and exclusion. He felt so dismal that to his final shame he burst into sobs. Zoe, who had been lying silent on the linoleum, turned quickly towards him and cradling his head against her breasts, stroked his hair and murmured, 'It's all right, darling. Everything will be all right.'

11

But of course when Jackson rejoined the unit everything was
not all right.

He missed Zoe agonisingly physically and, worse,
emotionally. Fortunately he very seldom met Christopher
Reid. The unit had all its three batteries in one place and the
officers ate together in a regimental mess at which once a
week there was a formal night (tunics, collars and ties) with
Mr Vice, usually the regimental orderly officer of the day,
proposing the loyal toast before the port circulated. Jackson
was posted as the third, or section, officer in J Troop which
Shannahan commanded with a monosyllabic Scotsman, later
transferred to another regiment, as the Gun Position Officer.
Reid was a GPO in another battery; Jackson never saw Reid
in the daytime and he took good care never to sit beside him
at mess. One lunchtime Reid came and sat down beside
Jackson and said pleasantly, 'How are you settling in? Zoe
mentioned you in a couple of letters — said you came round
for a bit of grub during the bridge-building course. She's a
great one for a party.' Jackson, his eyes riveted to his plate,
grunted something and Reid went on imperturbably, 'She's
taken a job in some sort of hospital auxiliary.'

To complicate everything, Jackson fell foul of the CO.

Lieutenant Colonel B. R. T. Yates, a prosperous wool-
broker in private life, was a thunderous black-haired man of
forty-two or forty-three who later won a DSO; he was given
to abrasive comments delivered in a voice so loud he was
nicknamed The Roarer. He made no secret of his belief that
reinforcement officers were an abomination; the wastage of
officers should be made up by taking good sergeants with

overseas experience out of the units and sending them to OTC. Of course the Army did this, but it could not find enough NCOs with the education needed for technical units such as the artillery or the engineers. Nevertheless, The Roarer received Jackson sourly on his first night in the mess. Jackson dreaded having to show himself in front of all the veterans. When he entered the hut being used as the mess he made the mistake of going up to Shannahan, the only familiar face, and saying hullo. The Roarer, standing drink in hand at the bar, said loudly to his second in command, 'They don't teach these new boys much military etiquette these days.'

'Oh, Jesus!' muttered Shannahan. 'You're supposed to go up to the senior officer present and say good evening to him before you speak to anybody else.' Jackson, his face burning, stood to attention in front of The Roarer and said, 'Good evening, sir.' The Roarer merely turned his back, growling, 'Bit bloody late.'

A few days later Jackson was rostered as Regimental Orderly Officer. Notebook in hand he joined a comet consisting of the colonel, the second in command, the captain quartermaster, the doctor, the orderly sergeant and a runner, which wound its way through the lines. Jackson found that The Roarer knew the name of any soldier of any rank whom he met. He roared at the troops, but they seemed to enjoy it. In the RHQ cookhouse, the inspection party discovered Alf Dugan, the sergeant cook, stirring a mixture of something in a huge iron pot. Dugan, pointing his dripping ladle at The Roarer's entourage, said, 'Jesus, colonel, if I'd known you was all coming I'd have made some scones.'

'Never mind the comedy!' bellowed The Roarer. 'What's in that pot there?'

'Sausages, sir,' said Dugan, a red-haired veteran of the shearing sheds.

The Roarer peered at the pot. 'They look like turds, Dugan.'

Dugan peered into the pot, too, and said, 'Bugger me, Colonel, I might have got me pots mixed. Anyway, we'll soon find out.'

'What do you mean?'

'This stuff is dinner for the officers' mess,' said Dugan.

'Christ!' said The Roarer. Shaking his head he led his acolytes out of the cookhouse. At the door he paused and bellowed, 'And put on a clean singlet, Dugan.'

'Very good, sir,' said Dugan, feeling, like The Roarer, that the morning had not been wasted.

Jackson found the gunners reasonably tolerant. They did what Jackson told them without arguing, although often he caught a look of amusement on their faces. Among the gunners were several examples of the wartime phenomenon of the well-educated and often well-to-do man who refused all promotion and thus avoided all responsibility. In J Troop there were three or four of these, two educated at King's, who called Jackson 'sir', but spoke to him in tones of offhand equality. Each of the key NCOs of the troop, the four gun sergeants who wore above their three stripes the coveted brass replica of a field gun, was boss of his own little kingdom — a gun, a limber, a tractor, a crew and a tent — and they did not let Jackson forget it. J Troop even had a classic example of an army stereotype, the Pommy Whinger. This was Gunner Knowes, Q. T., a gaunt Englishman of uncertain age who had served as a regular in the British Army and was known in the troop as 'The Perfect Soldier' because he effortlessly arranged his person, uniform and kit in regulation order, but was too stupid to become a gunlayer. Remaining an ammunition number, he devoted his time to criticising everything about the officers, the senior NCO and the Army. He had perfected the art of muttering comments to some other gunner just loud enough for an officer or NCO not to hear. Jackson had several irritating clashes with The Perfect Soldier, but his major trouble came from Troop Sergeant Major Docker.

From the start, Docker adopted a not-quite-offensive attitude towards Jackson, constantly emphasising his own years in the Regular Army. Weeks of tension finally climaxed when, during a morning parade, Jackson had the men brought to port arms so that he could inspect the barrels of the rifles artillerymen somewhat unwillingly carried. Jackson was surprised to see Docker, following behind him as required, merely to assist, looking down the barrels of rifles Jackson had already inspected. He said loudly to one man whose rifle Jackson had just seen and passed, 'There's rust down there, gunner! Get it clean today.' Jackson, controlling his temper, said to Docker, 'It won't be necessary for you to inspect any more rifles, Sar-Major. I'll do it.'

'It's not always easy to see rust, sir,' replied Docker. 'It takes a bit of experience to pick it.'

'Fall out, Sergeant Major,' Jackson said. 'I won't need you any further.'

'But sir —' Docker started to protest.

'Fall out, Sergeant Major. I'll handle this inspection myself.'

Docker, lips pursed in anger, stomped off parade. An hour later Shannahan said to him, 'Fucking Docker is carrying on about some run-in you had this morning. He's insisted on parading himself to Wilko to complain, so be prepared for a summons.'

It came that afternoon, not to the battery office but to Wilkinson's tent. He told Jackson to sit down, sighed, and said, 'George, this is the sort of fuss the battery can easily do without.'

'I'm sorry, sir,' Jackson said. 'It's just that Docker is continually trying to make me look small.'

'I know Docker,' said Wilkinson. 'I'm not going to amplify it but you can rely on it that I know exactly the sort of man Docker is. But subalterns get nowhere putting on a public confrontation. Of course, you were both in the wrong: Docker was being officious, looking down the barrels, and you shouldn't have ordered him off the parade like that.'

'But I didn't feel I could stand there and let him make a fool of me about missing a bit of rust.'

'You shouldn't have missed the rust in the first place.'

'I didn't see it, sir, to be truthful.'

'That's your fault. You're supposed to see it.'

'That's true,' said Jackson, feeling deflated.

'You will make a good officer, George,' said Wilkinson,

'but you are trying too hard. Just let the Army flow over you. It's a bit like what they say about rape. If you can't escape it, relax and enjoy it.'

'Very good, sir,' said Jackson.

Wilkinson added shrewdly, 'You needn't feel ashamed of being a reinforcement officer. What's your number — 30 000 something? That's pretty respectable. The battery captain is a reo. Joined us in Egypt. You'll be one of the mob as soon as you hear your first angry shot and that mightn't be all that far away.'

It turned out as the omniscient Wilkinson had said. After the battle against the Japanese, Jackson could join as an equal in the endless recountings and recallings of what had happened on this day or that night. Jackson felt as though he had spent his life with the battery; whenever he thought of the civilian world, it was an insider giving a passing glance at the outside. He no longer thought of himself as a law student; his profession had become artillery officer. His daily task was to keep the training going. His small talk concerned the dreary food, the heat, the tinea, the irregular mail from home and of course the endless flow of latrine rumours about what was going to happen to the battery. And when some real event occurred to break the monotony it was rarely pleasant.

82 Battery, still the only field artillery on the island, was deployed so that J Troop was well back from the jetty and able to put down fire on the water there or, by a quick swing of the line of guns, on adjoining beaches. K Troop's guns were sited in a spot from which they could cover two places on the track down from the tip of the island. A sergeant, a bombardier and eight gunners lived in two tents at each gun position. The signallers daily patrolled and tested the phone lines to the OPs and everything was inspected at least once daily by an officer. The remainder of the two troops and battery headquarters lived in the plantation midway between the two gun positions. The battery command post, known as the brain chamber, was there, dug into a big sandbagged bunker covered with a tarpaulin.

Occasionally each troop fired a few parsimonious rounds to check the registration of their emergency targets; everybody welcomed this as a relief from the boredom. Even more occasionally the exercise was done as a link shoot when the observer in one observation post brought all eight guns of the battery to bear on a single target after a good deal of artillery-board work in the battery command post. One afternoon, when Mailey was to do a link of a few rounds per gun, Jackson's bombardier assistant was acting as GPO of J Troop, Jackson was the gunlayer on Number 4 gun (closely watched by the sergeant to make sure he knew how to do it), some drivers were acting as ammunition numbers and Reid, looking almost dispirited, was wandering about behind the guns checking their line with his prismatic compass. The order to fire one round of gunfire came and Jackson noticed that the piercing bark of the guns was overlaid by an even shriller CR-A-A-CK. Out of the corner of his eye he saw a brilliant flash of light somewhere near him. Something went 'ping' against the breech block just behind his back and, looking down, he saw a small piece of metal on the muddy grass beneath his feet. He recognised it as a bit of shell casing and, turning in alarm to look along the line of guns, was just in time to see the loading number on the next gun fall slowly backwards and land on his back, watched openmouthed by the rest of the crew. There had been a premature explosion of the shell which had gone off, not when it hit the ground at the target, but a few feet after it had left the barrel of the gun. A large piece of the shell casing had hit Lance Bombardier Collins.

Reid reached him first.

The whole front of his shirt was drenched in blood. When Reid ripped it open Jackson saw that Collins' stomach had become a mass of unidentifiable organs churned into a red stew. Collins died as Jackson bent over him.

The crew of Collins' gun, white with shock, began to cluster around the body and a couple of the crew of the next gun started to run over.

66

'Stand fast!' Reid shouted. 'All crews take post! Richards, report troop out of action.'

The layers sank back on their seats, the other numbers knelt slowly down in their positions. Reid and the gun sergeant carried Collins' body back behind the command post and Reid reported what had happened over the phone to Battery.

'George,' he said. 'Stay with the body. Richards, tell the OP the troop has returned to action.' Not waiting for any replies, Reid walked to the Number 3 gun and took up the dead man's position on the left of the trail. Jackson saw Reid shove the shell up the breech. The brass cartridge case glinted momentarily as it was pushed up after the shell. The sergeant's arm went up over his head, signalling 'Ready'. When Richards rather shrilly shouted 'Fire!' several men in the crews tried to huddle as best they could behind the gun shields, but Reid took a couple of paces back so that he was standing well in the open. The sergeant motioned to him to step behind the shield but Reid ignored him. All guns fired without incident and the shells express-trained away over the trees to whumph down wherever they were going. When, after very depressing arrangements had been made about Collins' body, Jackson ventured some hesitant comment, Reid merely said, 'It's like an aircraft crash. They reckon it's best for survivors to fly again as soon as possible or they lose their nerve ...'

Sergeant Major Docker, nose shinier than ever, said, 'Don't you think, sir, it would have been wiser if you had stopped the shoot, withdrawn the ammunition on the gun site and had some fresh shells brought up?'

Jackson saw Reid's involuntary frown of irritation, but he replied evenly, 'Yes, Sergeant Major, I did consider that but new ammunition would have been in no better condition than the stuff we were using. Obviously everything deteriorates in this climate.'

'Well, I don't know,' said Docker. 'In the Regular Army —'

Reid paused a moment to control himself.

'I don't think you grasp the position, Sergeant Major,' he said. 'You are now in the only army that counts.'

Docker affected disbelief. 'You can't be serious, sir,' he said.

'I am perfectly serious,' said Reid. 'We are the real army — the wartime amateurs. Us. The civilians suddenly asked to be soldiers when a war breaks out. We do the fighting.'

Docker was speechless with indignation.

'And you regulars,' Reid added, 'are merely the caretakers. You just look after the premises in peacetime.'

'Perhaps the amateurs would do better to profit by our experience,' Docker spluttered. 'And as to that ammunition, I've had a good deal to do with ammunition and my advice is —'

'Fuck your advice,' said Reid. 'Your experience with ammunition has probably been driving it around in a GS wagon. You and your advice are a bloody nuisance, Docker.'

Jackson was astounded. He had never heard Reid lose his temper before. In the chilling silence Docker, his lips pursed as though he had bitten on a lemon, tried to do a drill book about-turn, nearly fell over and marched stiffly away. Nobody was surprised to hear that Warrant Officer Class 2 Docker, G. L., had paraded himself to the CO to complain that Captain C. R. Reid had spoken to him abusively in the presence of others. In the upshot Wilkinson ticked both men off. Reid held out his hand to Docker, who took it with such ill grace that there could be no mistaking his enmity. The battery voted in its own way. Jackson was taking Atebrin parade a couple of days later when Reid walked past; a murmur of affection ran through the line of men and Jackson heard Gunner Hodges (a Queensland canecutter nicknamed The Pineapple because of his roughness) mutter to a neighbour, 'No doubt about that fuckin' Tut — he's a bottler, ain't he?' Jackson passed on this accolade to Reid, expecting him to laugh, but Reid merely said sadly, 'None of this nonsense brings Collins back. He had only been married a year. My God, I hate it when something like this happens.'

Various tropical diseases niggled away at all the units on the island. There was a big drive on the pools of water in which the anopheles mosquito bred and men could be seen plodding about everywhere with knapsack sprayers. A village of Sarunian natives was inhabited again in a clearing a couple of miles from the jetty. Jackson went down there once and saw, among the thatched huts on stilts, bare-breasted women in grass skirts followed by sickly toddlers born with malaria and showing the swollen abdomen caused by an enlarged spleen. The Army had tried to use the men, all with magnificent balloons of lice-filled hair, to dig drains to carry off surplus water from the plantations into the creeks which ran through the area, but disgusted NCOs found that the men only worked for twenty minutes at a time before they dropped their shovels and sat down. At first everybody talked about lazy bastards of fuzzy wuzzies, but it soon became clear that endemic malaria had made the men too weak to do any sustained work.

The Royal Australian Army Medical Corps seemed to have unbounded faith in the ability of Atebrin to suppress malaria and the force commander concluded that if men continued to report sick with malaria they had either been forgetting to take the little yellow wonder pills or had deliberately not been taking them in the hope of being sent back to hospital on the mainland. The brigadier was aware, too, of the old rumour that Atebrin made you sterile (or was it impotent?); as nobody was clear as to the difference, many an inconclusive argument, with much hearsay evidence adduced, raged through the men's tents. The brigadier had it made widely known that a man had to be dying of something to be sent back to the mainland; malaria cases merely went into the grimmish field hospital not far from the airstrip. Still the malaria cases continued. The brigadier, thumping his fist on his table in the old manager's house he used as force headquarters, said, 'Well, bugger it! We'll have Atebrin taken by numbers.' Thus was instituted a bizarre ceremony.

The troops had long ago been ordered to wear shirts,

with sleeves rolled down, and boots and gaiters, as soon as the sun went down and the anopheles came out. Now every evening meal parade of every unit or sub-unit had to be attended by an officer carrying a large tin of Atebrin and flanked by a warrant officer or senior NCO with a roll of the men's names. Each man had to have his mug half full of water. As he came to the mess orderlies serving the food each soldier received, in his hand, from the officer, his two little yellow tablets. In view of the officer, the man had to place the tablets on his tongue and take a drink from his mug to wash the tablets down. His name was then ticked on the roll. In a K Troop queue one gunner remarked more voce than sotto, 'Jesus, the skulls will be round checking which hand you wipe your arse with next.' Captain Mailey, the plump ever-smiling ex-accountant who commanded the troop heard this and grinningly replied, 'No, I won't, Gunner Higgs — I'll be looking to see if you use any paper,' which sent the whole troop into roars of laughter and shouts of 'Stop using your finger, Higgsy!'

Jackson found it disturbing to have to watch grown men stick out their tongues but he soon got used to it. Reid found it harder. Coming back from a mess parade once he said, 'It's bloody disgusting having to look down all those throats.'

At the evening meal in the officers' tent a couple of weeks later, Jerry Taylor, the Command Post Officer, a balding, stocky man close to forty, looked at the plate of food put before him by Davis, once more on duty as mess orderly, and said, 'What's this, Whacker?'

'It's zebu,' said Whacker. 'I should have warned all you gents. They've slaughtered some of them local zebu and issued them as rations.'

'You don't mean those tough old hump-back animals you see wandering about the plantation?'

'That's them,' said Whacker. 'Zebu.'

Athol Honeysett, who, as Battery Captain, was its second in command and housekeeper, had well known what was in the dixies. He hastily interposed, 'Well, it's fresh meat, anyway. Someone at brigade thought it would make a change from tinned stuff.'

'Bloody silly idea,' said a deep, deep voice. It came from the tall, black-haired, hawk-nosed lieutenant named Bolton who was now Wagon Lines Officer. 'Animals are all muscle.'

Reid took a couple of mouthfuls and pushed his plate away. 'I just can't eat this,' he said.

'Close your eyes, Chris,' said Honeysett. 'Doesn't taste so bad when you can't see it.'

'Lot of the men can't eat it, either,' said Bolton. 'They'd rather have bully and biscuits.'

'That so, Whacker?' Wilkinson asked.

'Dead right, sir. Any of you gents want a drink of my special?' He poured out a few glasses of a passionfruit cordial mixed with warm water. Jackson found it tasted more strongly than ever of chlorine. Reid took a sip and put down the thick glass tumbler.

'The zebu isn't the worst of it,' he said. 'It's the dehydrated potatoes and dehydrated cabbage — Christ, talk about the horrors of war!'

'I seen a ship unloading at the wharf this morning,' said Davis. 'You'd think they'd send us up some fresh food.'

'Nothing in it but medical supplies and ammunition,' said Honeysett. An actuary in private life, he was a fit, plain man who wore steel-rimmed issue spectacles.

When everybody had either forced down a little zebu, or spat it out as inedible gristle, Wilkinson rapped on the table and said, 'If you don't mind, I just want to talk a little business. I was summoned to Barnum and Bailey's this morning for a chat with the ringmaster and our learned colleagues from the aeroplane preservation society.'

'The 3.7 mob?' asked Taylor, surprised.

'None other,' said Wilkinson. 'Somebody has pointed out to the Brig that from our defensive positions our 25-pounders cannot reach the tip of the island and if ever the Nips came back here it might be very unwise for us to try to get guns up that track to bring fire down on those little beaches right at the top. However, the anti-aircraft guns near the strip have a range considerably greater than ours and if they depressed their barrels and fired on land they could hit those northern beaches from right where they are now.'

'I feel there's a but,' said Reid.

'Dead right. The but is that the ack-ack mob have no contact fuses. Lots of time-set airburst fuses, but nothing to make their lovely shells go off if they bounce against a Japanese skull. On the other hand, some genius reminded the Brig that 25-pounder batteries use contact fuses all the time. Wouldn't it be nice if our fuses fitted the ack-ack shells, he said.'

'Well, bugger me,' rumbled Bolton who was responsible for the maintenance of the battery's vehicles and ammunition reserves. Despite the saturnine maturity of his face, he was unmarried and strangely innocent of the world outside his Rugby League club. The gunners had nicknamed him 'Baby'.

'The guts of it,' Wilkinson said, 'is that we have been ordered to discover if our fuses will screw into ack-ack shells. After all, our calibre is 3.3 inches and theirs is 3.7 so Ordnance may have given us the same fuse holes. Anyway, if our stuff does it, we have to give the ack-ack mob two hundred of our fuses right away.'

'But we don't have any loose fuses,' said Honeysett. 'The brigadier must know all our fuses are screwed into the noses of shells.'

'Of course he knows that. He expects the fuses to be unscrewed and taken up to the ack-ack mob, who in return will unscrew their fuses which we will bring back and screw into the noses of our shells.'

'Well, bugger me,' rumbled Baby again.

There was a small silence. Everybody knew that under the best of conditions screwing and unscrewing fuses was a hobby to be avoided. Fuses had more than one in-built safety device, but, if they failed, the detonating charge of the fuse, which was intended to activate the main explosive inside the shell, could itself do a lot of damage.

Mailey, not smiling for once, said, 'Who knows what our stuff's like after lying around in this climate? That prem that killed your gunner, Chris, that was a faulty fuse.'

'I know,' Wilkinson said, 'and I've put this to the brigadier, but he sticks by the book and says the safety devices are supposed to be foolproof, so get on with it. However, I propose that the job be done by volunteers. Hands up who wants to take charge of the screwing, if you'll excuse the expression.'

Almost impatiently Reid interrupted, 'There's no need for all this, Tim. I should look after this fuse nonsense. I did the ammunition course in Cairo, remember?'

'Is that where you were?' said Mailey. 'I thought you were in the pox hospital.' He turned to Wilkinson. 'Chris is only trying to show off his superior knowledge. I'll do the fuses.'

'Or I will,' said Honeysett.

Wilkinson thought for a moment.

'It's appreciated,' he said, 'but I think I'll accept Chris' offer. There's just a chance he's still got his notes. How many offsiders do you want, Chris?'

'Oh, a couple, maybe three.'

'I'll ask each troop and battery HQ to call for one volunteer then,' said Wilkinson. 'Are we having a little game tonight or aren't we?'

It was soon found that, through a rare feat of industrial standardisation, the 25-pounder fuses would indeed thread into the tops of 3.7 shells. So a working party built Reid a little bunker well away from the tents, and shells from Baby's reserves were brought down ten or a dozen at a time. Reid and his little party unscrewed the fuses gingerly, starting them with the little pronged tool, and finally unscrewing them slowly with their fingers and placing them on beds of rags in empty ammunition boxes which were then driven (very slowly) to the anti-aircraft battery where an equal number of strange-looking fuses from their shells were picked up, brought back and screwed into the empty holes. Wilkinson wandered down a couple of times and sat inside the bunker chatting and unscrewing a few fuses himself. So did Jackson, concealing his trepidation. He had only just left the bunker on the last day of the job when he heard the crump of an explosion followed by a long wailing cry of pain and fear. He leaped back to find that a fuse had gone off right in a young bombardier's hand, reducing it to something like red spaghetti. Nobody else had been touched. Reid had already whipped the belt off his slacks and put it on the boy's arm as a tourniquet.

Wilkinson was down at the jetty at the time, but Honeysett materialised in his place and abruptly ordered an end to the whole fuse transferring exercise. Reid drove the barely conscious boy to the field hospital. He waited until the doctor had seen him and decided that if he were flown back to the mainland at once expert surgery might save two of his fingers but not his thumb. When Reid came back to the troop office he looked white and strained.

'Of course it would be Halliday's right hand,' he said to Jackson. 'He's a draughtsman by occupation. What an insensate waste! And all because some prick at Brigade wants to make himself look smart.' Reid hurled his hat down on the table. 'Bullshit!' he shouted, 'Bullshit! The Japs are never going to come back to Saruna. They won't waste time on another attack on this malaria-ridden little pimple. They'll attack Moresby, but meantime you and I and everybody else are stuck forever in this mind-numbing boredom footling about with ammunition that obviously can't stand the climate. First there was the prem on our gun and now a fuse goes off in Halliday's hand — does nobody ever learn?'

Reid was breathing heavily and sweating profusely around the face although it was nearly evening.

'Are you OK, Chris?' Jackson asked. 'You're not getting malaria, are you?'

'Oh, Christ! Is that all you can say?' Reid muttered and half stumbled out of the office towards his own tent.

12

Reid stayed in bed for the next two days, looking ill and apparently sleeping most of the time, although once when Jackson walked past the tent he saw him sitting up staring into space with a peculiar concentration. When Reid was up again he was gaunt, but in manner he seemed the old imperturbable Tutankhamen once more. Coming into Reid's tent a week later, Jackson found him, slide rule in one hand and pen in the other, covering a page of paper with mathematical equations.

'Working out a new way to cook dehydrated turnips?' Jackson asked.

'Just trying to see how much physics I remember,' Reid answered. 'I can feel my brain turning into sludge here.'

Jackson thought no more about it. People killed the endless hours in various ways. The men had put in a good deal of time raising their sleeping tents three or four feet off the ground on platforms with palm tree trunks as corner posts and bamboo stems as slatted floors; this was certainly much cooler. Every man had made himself a rough stretcher consisting of a blanket or a hessian bag slung between two poles. The men lived six or eight to a tent; officers lived one or two to a tent, on their portable, fold-up stretchers. But no matter how much housekeeping was done or how repetitively the equipment was maintained, there always seemed to be many spare hours in a day and the great Army time-sponge of route marching was out of the question in the heat.

With the help of a nearby RAEME light engineering detachment, several gunners industriously turned Australian bayonets of dubious provenance into Japanese commando knives and sold them to American airmen at the strip as having been found near a body in the jungle. Many gunners played euchre, rummy, cribbage, auction bridge, contract bridge and chess. An art student who later became a leading portrait painter did wonderful sketches of the camp scenes. Several gunners studied for future law exams. A gun crew, having acquired some copper tubing from the wreck of a Kittyhawk which had crashed in the jungle near the strip, constructed a crude but effective still with which they made a hell-fire alcoholic brew from whatever raw material was handy; dried apricots from the rations were a favourite.

Several men kept illegal diaries for some sort of book they vaguely imagined they would write after the war. A signaller who was a jujitsu expert conducted a small class which put a driver in hospital with a dislocated shoulder. But to Jackson's knowledge only one man in the battery passed his time with mathematical exercises and that was Reid. It was logical enough. He was after all a mathematician and he had always carried a couple of text books as well as some sets of tables which made Army-issue log tables for artillery use look like a child's guide to counting.

There had always been a fair air of tolerant mockery about many things Reid said; he called Routine Orders, Part I, the Old Testament and Part II the New Testament. He called the guns the jujus — 'What else? They are sacred objects which we worship with a series of strange rites.' To Docker's disgust J Troop parades under Reid had developed a peculiarly discursive character. After all the shouting about 'Right Section all present and correct' and 'Left Section, two duties, two sick, otherwise all present and correct' and the issue of the day's orders, Reid would usually ask, 'Does anybody wish to say anything?' Sometimes a man would make a complaint or suggestion which Reid would listen to carefully. Sometimes this would lead to a sort of debate in which several people joined. Reid often made a wry comment at which everyone laughed.

Consequently nobody thought much about it when Reid asked at one parade, 'Has anybody here got a thermometer?'

A driver had a clinical thermometer in his roll of toilet gear and Reid arranged to borrow it. Its use became apparent a few days later when Jackson found Reid conducting an experiment on the grass behind his tent. He had propped up his shaving mirror at an angle which delivered a spot of light on a small glass half-filled with water in which stood the thermometer. 'Hold this a minute, will you?' Reid asked, giving Jackson one end of a length of rope. 'Put it down immediately in front of the mirror.' Reid ran the rope to the glass and tied a knot in the rope there. 'I'll measure the distance exactly later,' he said.

'What's all this about?' Jackson asked.

'This is a very crude check on the amount of heat a mirror can deliver to an object at a certain distance by reflecting the very hot sunlight at this latitude at eleven o'clock in the morning. I'll tell you more later — I'm still calculating.'

In the following days Reid covered page after page with calculations and several times went to various clearings in the jungle and carefully paced out the distance from one side of it to the other. He went down to the RAEME detachment and had a discussion with the captain in charge of it. Then he went through the battery's nominal roll, found a signaller who was a glazier in civil life and had a long conversation with him, after which the man reported to his mates, 'Buggered if I know what Tut's up to — he kept asking me how they made glass and I couldn't tell him too much because I used to spend my time fixing up broken window panes.' Reid made another visit to RAEME. Jackson noted that even after that short walk, Reid was out of breath and sweated heavily.

A couple of days later Wilkinson, who, as usual, seemed to know everything, dropped into the J Troop office and off-handedly asked, 'What are all the abstruse calculations about, Chris?'

'The objective is simple,' Reid said. 'I think we can harness an omnipresent natural resource as a useful sup-plementary weapon. We have had some very nasty experiences with ammunition which has been affected by the heat and humidity here. Obviously we would reduce these episodes if we fired fewer rounds and we could fire fewer rounds if we could introduce an auxiliary weapon to the battle scene.' He went to the door of the tent and pointed to the sky. 'That's what can help us — the sun. We should be harnessing the enormous energy the sun delivers free daily.'

'But how?' Wilkinson asked.

'Through mirrors, of course,' said Reid. 'Many experiments have been made overseas in which the sun's rays picked up by specially designed reflectors have been concentrated on a container of water which has been brought to the boil and produced steam very quickly. You know yourself that if you focus the sun on your hand even with a cheap little pocket magnifying glass, you cannot stand the heat for more than a few seconds. My calculations suggest that if we had proper mirrors for use in the field we could direct beams of light from one side of a jungle clearing to the other and cause havoc among the Japanese assembled there. We would either burn their faces and arms and cause them to pull back, or temporarily blind them or even set the undergrowth on fire in some places.'

Jackson, puzzled, glanced at Wilkinson to see his reaction. Wilkinson, poker-faced, said, 'I see. How big would these mirrors be?'

'Oh, maybe this big,' said Reid holding his hands above his head.

'Do you think Japanese riflemen might riddle them with bullets as soon as they saw them?'

'Ah, ha,' said Reid, triumphantly. 'I've thought of that. I've been talking to the engineer types at RAEME and they say it would be simple to mount the mirrors on a swivel so you could turn them edge on towards the Japs to make a target very, very hard to hit, until you were ready to swing them round and beam the rays at the Nips. No, that's not the problem. The important thing is to calculate the size and curvature of the mirror surface to deliver the maximum concentration of light. I've got as far as rough calculations, but the final work will have to be done in a physics laboratory back on the mainland. When I've got a few notes together I thought I'd come and see you and we could talk about it further.'

Reid flopped down on the bench and mopped his face.

'I see,' said Wilkinson. 'Very interesting. And how have you been yourself? You're looking a bit grim.'

'Nothing wrong with me,' said Reid. But he did in fact look ill. His face seemed to have become narrower, his forehead higher and his eyes more deeply sunken beneath his corn-coloured eyebrows.

'I must push off,' Wilkinson said. 'Don't forget miniature ranging for all officers at ten hundred tomorrow near our mess tent. You're orderly officer, aren't you, George? Will you bring a blanket and the cotton wool thing and so on?'

'Very good, sir,' said Jackson. Reid merely nodded absently.

Miniature ranging needed very little equipment — a blanket to represent a landscape with some boots under it to make hills, various odds and ends scattered about on it to represent buildings, bridges and so on, and a long stick with a blob of cotton wool stuck on the end of it. One by one, the officers were called on to engage various types of target described as offering on the landscape. The officer doing the shoot sat a few yards back from the blanket in an imaginary observation post with his imaginary guns somewhere behind him and called out real fire orders. An officer using the long stick placed the cotton wool, representing a shell burst, at the spot where the rounds had landed; he used a few secret chalk marks around the end of the blanket to indicate yards from the gun position and degrees to either side of the zero line running from the gun position approximately through the centre of the terrain. Fire orders had to be given in their immutable sequence: number of guns to be employed, ammunition, azimuth expressed as degrees to the left or right of the zero line, angle of sight, ranging instructions if needed range in yards, number of rounds, type of fire.

Miniature ranging was an essential ingredient in the life

of an artillery officer; it was the device by which he kept in training for his paramount duty, the directing of fire upon enemy targets of all types. Wilkinson once told the mess, 'I reckon that in the Australian Army every rank does the work which should be done by one rank lower — sergeants do bombardiers' work, subalterns do sergeants' work and so on. The British army has learned better. Those chubby cheeked subalterns probably don't know half their men's names, but they have been drilled until they can engage any sort of target in their sleep. They realise that if they do that they can leave the NCOs to run the troop.'

For the miniature ranging, Jackson spread the blanket in the shade of a palm tree, fixed the props and, saluting formally, handed over to Wilkinson. Wilkinson, taking the cotton wool stick himself, said, 'All set? Right, we'll start with some conventional targets in that well-known fairytale open countryside and then we'll get in touch with reality with some jungle-type close targets. First shoot: observer Captain Reid, critic Captain Mailey. Chris — church with steeple, right, two o'clock, four fingers, farm house.'

Reid raised his binoculars and after a long pause, re-plied, 'Seen.'

'A battalion or so of enemy infantry is reported to have dug in across the paddocks between the farmhouse and the cross roads. Seen?'

Again the long pause while Reid searched with his binoculars.

'Our infantry has asked us to tickle up these enemy troops. Go to it.'

It was an easy shoot at a big stationary target, the sort of thing any of the officers could have rattled off. Reid started automatically, 'Troop target, charge two —' and lowered his binoculars. He wiped the eyepieces with a hand-kerchief and began again. 'Troop target, charge two, right ranging —' Knowing this was an error of sequence he muttered, 'Oh, shit!' put his glasses down and wiped his face. The sweat was falling off the end of his nose in droplets.

'Are you OK?' asked Ramsay, K Troop's small, quizzical Gun Position Officer, a surveyor in civil life.

'Of course I'm OK,' Reid answered shortly. 'It's just bloody hot. I say again: Troop target, charge two, zero, right, eight degrees . . .' He stumbled through to the end of the fire order.

Wilkinson plopped the cotton wool down at the spots corresponding to Reid's fire orders and it was immediately obvious he had made a beginner's error by dropping both his opening ranging shots on the far side of the target instead of bracketing one over and one short and halving this bracket, several times if need be, until he was on the target. The same bracketing system was supposed to be used to get the line correct, but Reid made a reckless simultaneous correction to both his line and range and put down two further rounds both minus of the target and way off line. It took him a long time to blunder to the target after a dreadful shoot. Mailey, as critic, smiled his way through a few stock phrases and sat down as soon as he could. Everybody felt embarrassed about the whole thing, for Reid was known as a quick and effective fire director.

Afterwards Wilkinson took Reid on one side and said, 'I think you've got malaria.'

'I don't have any shivering,' said Reid.

'You're taking your Atebrin, aren't you?' Wilkinson asked. 'You're not vomiting it up or anything?'

'No, I hold it down all right,' Reid said. 'Don't have much appetite though.'

The next week Reid spent more and more time in his tent, turning through his couple of text books and calculating. 'I wish I had a decent book on the physics of light,' he told Jackson, 'but just from the stuff I've got here I'm sure the mirror idea is feasible. I've reached the stage when I should do something practical about it.'

'Such as what?' Jackson asked.

'Such as having a couple of mirrors built and put to field tests.'

'Could RAEME make them?'

'RAEME? Never. They're great on a bit of rough welding but the mirror would need some high-class work back on the mainland. I could give them the dimensions and curvatures at least for a trial model.'

The idea of field testing a full-sized mirror seemed to get hold of Reid, and shortly to obsess him. He started to talk about his mirrors to any officer who would listen. He began to bring pieces of paper covered with figures into the mess at night and pass them around the table while he delivered a harangue about the urgent necessity of getting a working model made and the need to get the High Command to interest itself in the alternative weapon.

Several officers pointed out to Reid that the whole idea was an absurdity. Even if a suitable mirror could be made, the problems of transporting it to a forward position and placing it so that it caught the sun's rays at the correct angle were very great. The thought of asking infantry to erect and adjust a mirror in full view of close Japanese riflemen was comical. Reid seemed deaf to all objections. He merely reiterated everything he had said and his volubility increased to a point at which officers scuttled out of the mess tent as fast they could to get away from him. The batmen doing duty as mess orderlies carried eyewitness acounts back to the lines. And Jackson noticed many gunners watching Reid closely as though they expected to see him do something odd.

Wilkinson privately asked Jackson, 'Does Chris carry on about his bloody mirror in the troop office, too?'

'He does a bit,' said Jackson.

'You don't think old Chris is gradually going off his rocker with cerebral malaria, do you?'

'Cerebral malaria?' said Jackson, surprised. 'I knew you could get gastric malaria but I haven't heard of cerebral malaria.'

'Man in one of the infantry companies went raving mad — they had to tie his hands and feet together to get him to hospital,' Wilkinson said. 'Their CO told me the poor bugger had been ranting on about writing a new national anthem for a couple of weeks.'

'Chris is not raving,' said Jackson, defensively.

'No?' said Wilkinson.

Being only part of a regiment, 82 Battery did not have its own doctor and as Reid had stubbornly refused suggestions that he should go to the field hospital for a check-up, Wilkinson decided to avoid a direct confrontation by bringing the mountain to Tutankhamen. He quietly went to the hospital and spoke to the CO, a grizzled, big-handed lieutenant colonel who in private life had a general practice in a Queensland farming town. He took the point and agreed to send one of his doctors down to take a meal with 82 Battery, ostensibly to check on Atebrin taking, but in fact to observe Reid.

The doctor who came down, very unwillingly, had been a fashionable Melbourne gynaecologist who rued the day he had volunteered to serve in an army which could find no better use for his highly honed talents than send him to some forgotten tropical outpost to treat tertian malaria and look at sore throats, an end of the body in which he had very little interest. He arrived at 82 Battery more than usually disgruntled because the CO of the field hospital, who was not a specialist at all, had taken him to task over not inspecting hospital hygiene more closely. There was, the gynaecologist felt, something wrong with a system which expected an FRCS, FRCOG, to peer down a hole in the ground half-filled with human excreta.

When Reid was introduced to the guest at the evening meal he seemed to pull himself together and although sweat poured off him as though he was in the shower, he said very little until he discovered the visitor was a doctor and therefore somebody with a little scientific training. Reid then outlined his mirror project, talking slowly as with a first-time pupil and sounding more rational than he had for a long while.

Reid tried to show the doctor some of the pages of calculations he had brought to the mess, but the doctor pushed them away and said, 'Too hard for a medico — explain it to me,' after which Reid delivered a very competent lecture on the physics of heat and light. Taking the doctor back to his tent after mess, Wilkinson said, 'Well, what do you think about Captain Reid?'

'He certainly doesn't look well,' said the doctor. 'He seemed to be sweating enormously. But then some men do. And then his nails are pink — no anaemia.'

'What do you think of his mental state?'

'Captain Reid seemed to me to be perfectly sane,' replied the doctor. 'Voluble, even excitable. But he feels he has an exciting idea. I heartily agree that the High Command should pay more attention to alternate weapons. It's very obvious this whole Army is run on a dreadfully hidebound system which, incidentally, results in valuable talent being wasted in futile positions.'

'Thank you, doctor,' said Wilkinson. 'I'll call your jeep.' To Honeysett later he said, 'Bloody quack seemed madder than poor old Chris. I'm sorry for those poor bastards in the hospital — he's probably treating them for prolapsed wombs.'

13

Soon after that Reid began to talk about his mirror to the men.

It started at one morning parade when, having stood the battery easy, he said, 'I want to tell you something. I'm working on a device which could have an important bearing on jungle warfare. I won't say any more now but anybody who wants further information can come to the battery office at eleven hundred and I'll explain further. Parade ... Fall out, Mr Jackson. Carry on, Sergeant Major.'

Docker, all four gun sergeants, the command and observation post assistants and half a dozen gunners came to the troop office at eleven hundred and were given what Jackson was coming to recognise as a speech repeated over and over again. At the end of it, the NCOs walked away in silence but a couple of the gunners nudged one another in the ribs and Jackson heard a guffaw of laughter.

Docker, unnecessarily coming to attention, said to Reid, 'May I ask a question, sir? Do you seriously regard any of this mirror idea as being practical?'

'For God's sake!' said Reid impatiently. 'Any bloody fool should be able to see it's practical.'

Docker stalked glowering from the tent.

Reid, absorbed in his dream world, soon began to leave more and more of the troop administration to Jackson so that he was becoming the de facto troop commander, daily making the small decisions about training or housekeeping. Docker, almost audibly sniffing, helped him as little as possible, apparently to demonstrate that he considered Captain Reid was shirking. Jackson found it simplest to leave Docker to his standard tasks of detailing men for fatigues, working parties, training or manning the gun positions and to take advice when he needed it from the gun sergeants. When he felt compelled to use his own judgement and ignore what had been suggested, his orders were obeyed without fuss. For almost every small crisis there seemed to be a precedent drawn either from standing orders or unit custom. Jackson felt he had never before properly understood how an army worked. My God! he thought — the corset is closing around me.

Coming back from mess one night, he found Reid (who had not been at the meal) in the troop office bashing away with two fingers on the old typewriter, muttering and cursing the machine.

'Don't you want any food?' Jackson asked.

'Not hungry,' said Reid.

'What are you typing?'

'Something important. I can't get Wilkinson to pay any serious attention to the mirror project and the war keeps dragging on. Doesn't anybody realise it's time to get some action?' In his agitation he knocked a pile of scribbled notes on the floor.

Picking them up, Jackson asked, 'How will you do that?'

'By submitting a formal outline of my proposal,' said Reid. 'I'm typing it now. I'm going to insist that Wilkinson sends it to the force commander.'

'I see,' said Jackson, unconsciously echoing one of Wilkinson's mannerisms. 'Do you think ...?'

'Do I think what?'

'Nothing,' said Jackson. 'Nothing. Just remember to eat something.'

Next day Reid took a long, erratically typed memo, interspersed with equations, to Wilkinson and demanded that it be sent to the force commander for immediate action. When Reid came back to the troop office his hands were shaking as though he had Parkinson's disease.

'How did it go?' Jackson asked.

'It didn't fucking go!' Reid shouted. He hurled his hat to the far corner of the tent and banged his fist on the table. 'It did not go. Wilkinson refused to send my message on to the brigadier. It's unbelievable! How in Christ's name are we going to get the mirrors tried out if I can't even get the calculations in the right hands?'

Soon after Reid had shambled away to his tent, the phone from battery headquarters rang. It was Honeysett.

'The great drama of sea transport goes on,' he said. 'Another shipload of dehydrated potato or something is due tomorrow. The battery has to supply thirty-five men to unload, so could I ask J Troop to supply fifteen men under a sergeant? Have them outside the battery office in your own transport at oh five thirty. The BSM will be in charge. I'll talk to you first thing tomorrow about eating arrangements.'

The ship which arrived, after an anxious thrash from Port Moresby at the maximum speed its protesting engine could produce, turned out to be the *Leeuwarden*, a small, old, single-screw freighter, named after a charming town in the north of the Netherlands, which had been tramping around the Dutch East Indies before the war. Like others, the Dutch captain escaped the oncoming Japanese by heading the ship south until it reached some port still in Allied hands. After this he, his crew and the *Leeuwarden* had been pressed into service running supplies to the Allied-held islands. The *Leeuwarden* tied up at the Saruna jetty at 7 a.m. and unloading went on all day. By nightfall the holds were still only half empty and a new working party from 82 Battery was sent down to take over. Night fell, without a moon. At eight o'clock Reid and Jackson went down to the jetty to see how the men were doing. The darkness was so intense that standing on the wharf Jackson could not even see the outline of the trees at the water's edge. The working parties were stumbling about by the light of a few shaded pressure lanterns. Jackson and Reid were about to leave when the whole scene was brutally transformed by a sudden glare of light. The ship, jetty, working party and beach were illuminated as if in some huge newspaper photo made with a gigantic flash. For a moment Jackson did not understand what had happened but Reid knew.

'Searchlight,' he said. At the top of his voice he shouted, 'Down! Everybody down!' and threw himself full length on the wooden planks of the jetty.

'It's a bloody Japanese destroyer,' he muttered. 'Sneaked up and turned on its searchlight. Hold your hat.'

Immediately afterwards Jackson heard the terrifying metal-to-metal WHANG! of an armour piercing projectile hitting the side of the *Leeuwarden*. Men on the jetty scattered in a mad rush. Some trampled others trying to get away. Others jumped, or were knocked, into the water. From the *Leeuwarden*'s holds came the shouts of the men trapped inside. The ship was a pathetically simple target for the six leisurely, well-aimed rounds drilled into her hull. The *Leeuwarden* sank the few feet down to the sea bottom and settled there, listing away from the wharf. The destroyer played its searchlight around the beach and fired another four or five rounds at random into the trees. Then it snapped off its searchlight and presumably steamed away at high speed, but any noise its engines made was hidden in the uproar of voices on the jetty.

The brigadier, a bald, portly, unmilitary-looking man who had survived the carnage of France in the First World War and won a DSO in the Second, came to the jetty himself half an hour later and stayed until dawn.

Seeing Wilkinson, who had arrived ten minutes after the noise of the firing had been heard in the 82 Battery lines, the brigadier ordered him to take charge of collecting the wounded. Two gunners had been killed, three more wounded and one man had broken a leg jumping off the jetty.

The night provided several incidents which passed into unit lore; one armour piercing round went right through both sides of the ship's hull, one actually stuck like a plug in the steel plates. A signaller in one hold escaped by climbing out the hole left by one round, fell into the water and nearly drowned. Honeysett was heading towards the jetty on foot when he was nearly knocked over by somebody running up the road the other way. Shining his torch Honeysett saw it was a man from some other unit who, having fallen over many times in his headlong flight, was covered from head to foot in a film of mud. Beneath he was wearing a shirt, boots and gaiters but no pants.

'Where are your trousers?' Honeysett asked.

'Here, of course,' panted the man. 'I was working in my shorts —' He looked down and said, amazed, 'Jesus Christ, where are my bloody strides?' He had somehow run right out of his pants.

The story spread through the battery in a few hours and everybody laughed, including Jackson, but he told nobody of the paralysing fright which had gripped him when the searchlight suddenly came on and caught him in its blinding glare at the end of the jetty. He had felt that he personally was the target at which the destroyer would start firing. He found later that many of the men had experienced the same feeling. But when he mentioned this to Reid, it had merely launched him into a tirade on the old theme: 'The lesson's clear. More men killed over ammunition. A lot of the *Leeuwarden*'s cargo was ammunition, you know, and men had to unload it. Why not investigate alternative weapons? There's my mirror to start with. But do you think I can get anybody here to pay attention? Wilkinson finally sent my calculations on to the brigadier and what happened? Nothing. I've had no answer. Some shitty little staff officer who couldn't understand them has wiped his bum on them. I can't get through to anybody on this island.'

They were talking in the troop office and Docker came in just as Jackson, hoping to calm Reid, said, 'Why don't you send your calculations direct to Allied HQ on the mainland?'

A strange cunning look passed over Reid's face.

'Now you're talking. I've been thinking that it's MacArthur who should be looking over my calculations. He may be a great publicity hound but he's a daring sort of general. I wouldn't expect him to be as hidebound as these bloody idiots here.'

'Well,' said Jackson, wanting to get away. 'Send MacArthur the papers direct. I expect it's a terrible breach of some sort of regulation, but desperate situations need desperate remedies.'

'Exactly my view,' said Reid. 'Exactly my view. Desperate action is needed.'

God knows what he's raving on about now, Jackson thought, but I wish somebody would realise he's gone off his rocker. Docker, at the table, said nothing. He kept his head bent over the clipboard.

14

An inspection of the *Leeuwarden* in daylight revealed even more bad news. Sitting full of holes on the bottom, it had permanently blocked one side of the jetty; the water on the other side was too shallow to take even a small freighter. The task of mooring a ship at sea off the port and bringing its cargo in by lighter was beyond the mechanical or human resources of the garrison. But then some of the far-away, never seen gods who controlled the lives of Allied outposts demonstrated that they did not spend all their time sipping ambrosia in the Deities' Mess; various Dakotas carrying hospital supplies fluttered down on the airstrip, followed by a B-18 chock-a-block with tinned food, and only four days after the *Leeuwarden* went down a businesslike diesel ketch about 75 feet long arrived and found enough water to tie up on the opposite side of the jetty. She carried in her small hold and on deck food, ammunition and, unbelievably, two pushbikes. The crew was all Polynesian; the skipper was a handsome Solomon Islander. The boat, it turned out, had been an island trading lugger before the war and it had slipped across from Port Moresby undetected by the Japanese Navy. A few days later a deep-sea tug came roaring up to the jetty loaded to the gunwales with supplies. Somebody seemed to be organising a small Dunkirk in reverse.

A week after the tug, another craft arrived. Ramsay, who had been down at the jetty with an unloading party, came back for lunch and told the mess, 'Well, they seem determined to keep us alive. No stone unturned.'

'The boat's brought some dancing girls?' Ramsay asked.

'Get your mind off sex. This boat came from the mainland and guess what? Half its cargo is genuine Aussie fresh potatoes.'

'How do you know?' Baby demanded.

'Because one of the gunners accidentally opened the corner of a sack with his knife and we saw what was inside. Look!' Ramsay fished in his pocket, dramatically, pulled out a potato and plonked it down on the mess table. Honeysett squeezed it, 'Good God,' he said. 'It's real.'

Reid, who had been sitting silent for once, took the potato in his hand and examined it carefully as though satisfying himself it was in good order.

'Where did this boat come from?' he asked.

'Broome,' said Ramsay.

'Big boat?'

'Two masts and a crew of assorted colours,' said Ramsay. 'I suppose you'd call it a lugger or a trader or something.'

'Where are they going after this?' Reid asked. 'Over to New Guinea, I suppose?'

'No, the skipper told me they are going straight back to the mainland to pick up more food for us. The skipper's like something out of Somerset Maugham. He's shit-scared of the Jap Navy, too.'

That afternoon when Jackson and Reid were alone in the troop office Reid said, 'You do appreciate the importance of my mirror, don't you, George?'

'Sure,' said Jackson. 'It's a very interesting idea.'

'No, no,' said Reid impatiently. 'Do you really understand that it's essential that my drawings and calculations get to the very top, right to MacArthur himself?'

'I know how you feel,' Jackson answered, his mind on something else. He had become so accustomed to lectures about the mirror that he no longer listened.

'But you do understand, don't you?' Reid persisted.

'Yes, of course,' Jackson answered mechanically.

At breakfast next morning Reid looked ghastly and he did not appear for lunch.

'Chris not feeling up to it?' Wilkinson asked.

'I haven't seen him for an hour or two,' Jackson said.

After mess Jackson went to the troop office and Reid's tent. He was in neither. Jackson rang J Troop gun position. Reid was not there, either. Feeling vaguely disturbed, Jackson went back to Reid's tent and was standing there wondering what to do next when he noticed that Reid's great sheaf of calculations were not on his table where he kept them. Nor, Jackson noticed, glancing quickly around, was Reid's canvas haversack, the handy small version of the backpack.

Don't tell me the poor devil has tramped off into the jungle, Jackson thought. Then a far more alarming idea came to him. He walked to his own tent, lay on his bed thinking for five minutes, got up, walked to the troop vehicle park, climbed into his vehicle, a Ford one-ton utility with a high canvas canopy over the back, and drove to the jetty. The most hackneyed of all artillery precepts came into his mind: 'Time spent in reconnaissance is seldom wasted.'

At the jetty he saw that the lugger from the mainland had rigged a single derrick to work cargo out of its one hold. The process of getting up a sling-load, hauling on the guys to swing the boom over the jetty, lowering the load and swinging the boom back inboard again seemed very slow. Jackson parked his vehicle in the palm trees and immediately saw Reid's vehicle, also parked there. It, too, was a one-ton utility with a canopy but with a big OJ painted on each door where Jackson, as GPO, had GJ. Jackson walked over; Reid was not in the truck or anywhere in sight but the keys were still in the ignition. On the front seat lay Reid's haversack, bulging full. Jackson hesitated a moment from embarrassment, but, realising what he had to do, he unbuckled the straps. In the haversack were one of Reid's spare shirts, a pair of slacks, a towel, a handkerchief, a pair of socks, some toilet paper, a tin mug, a packet of ration dog biscuits and Reid's square pigskin toilet case. If his razor's in it, I'll know for certain, Jackson thought. He undid the zipper which ran around three sides of the toilet case and the lid portion quickly hinged back to reveal a razor, shaving brush, cake of soap, hairbrush and comb, toothbrush, toothpaste and a pair of nail scissors. The haversack was packed with a complete emergency travelling kit.

You mad bastard, Jackson thought, angered. Now I suppose I'll have to go and search the lugger. He went to zip the toilet case together again when he noticed a square of white cardboard, cut to the exact size, wedged inside the lid. Jackson looked more closely; it was the back of a photographic print. Ashamed but unable to resist the urge, half guessing and half dreading what was on the other side, Jackson put a fingernail under the photo, prised it out of the case and turned it over.

The photograph, sharp and well-lighted, showed Zoe, naked, on the bed in the main bedroom in the house in Wahroonga. She was lying on her right side facing the camera, her head propped up on one hand while the other lay relaxed on her stomach. Beneath her elbow Jackson saw a pillow he recognised; Zoe had often stuffed it beneath her buttocks when she and Jackson had made love on that bed. Her big breasts had fallen a little downwards under their own weight and the aureoles looked huge. Zoe was smiling in invitation at the person who had taken the photograph and he, Jackson realised, could only be Reid. At the bottom of the photo Zoe had written in pen, 'I'm waiting, my darling — come back safely.'

Jackson felt so real and acute a physical pain that he put his hand to his side.

'Oh, shit,' he said, stupidly. 'Oh, shit, oh, shit . . .'

After a while he looked again at the body he knew so well, a body which, he realised, was not his, no matter how fully he had explored it. Reid had taken the photograph skilfully but the aura which arose from that black and white bromide came from the subject. The picture was deeply sensual; it seemed to transmit memories of private delights shared with Reid and be redolent with the promise of others to come. The inscription was not signed and did not even contain the conventional 'With love' or 'All my love' but Jackson comprehended at last that whether or not Zoe felt for her husband the emotion so commonly called love, she had spoken the truth — she was joined to Reid in some permanent way. And, worse, Jackson realised, he hungered for her himself.

Jackson was still holding the photograph when he heard a familiar noise, faint at first but growing louder. It came from the engine of one of the motorcycles with which artillery sergeant majors were issued. Glancing towards the road, Jackson saw the unmistakable shape of Docker, knees and elbows stuck out, riding towards the jetty. Jackson, galvanised, shoved the photograph back in the toilet case, crammed the case into the haversack and pushed the haversack to the floor; if Docker saw it, his curiosity would be endless. Docker dismounted and struggled, as usual, to get his bike up on its prop. Jackson strolled towards him.

'What brings you here, Sergeant Major?' he asked.

Docker finally managed to get the bike on the stand. 'Just looking,' he said. 'Keeping my eyes open.'

'For what?'

Docker drew off the great gauntlets he insisted on wearing no matter how hot the day. 'Captain Reid is here. I saw him drive away from the lines. This is his truck.'

'I know it's his bloody truck,' Jackson said impatiently. 'So what?'

'There's no need for Captain Reid to be here. The infantry is supplying this working party.'

'Stop a minute,' said Jackson. 'Captain Reid will go where he wishes. It's no concern of yours.'

Docker seemed to quiver with indignation.

'It does concern me!' he said. 'And all the men. We all know Captain Reid is dead keen to show those crazy calculations of his to somebody higher up. I've heard him say so myself. But it's Captain Reid's duty to stay here, like the rest of us, isn't it? I mean, why should he get out?'

All Jackson's alarm bells rang. Playing for time, he said, 'I don't quite follow your meaning.'

'Well, Captain Reid wouldn't be thinking of taking his calculations back personally, would he?'

'This is a peculiar conversation,' Jackson said, evenly. 'I

must be mistaken — you surely can't be suggesting that Captain Reid might go absent without leave, are you?'

Docker's big, sharp Adam's apple jumped up and down as he swallowed. He realised he had gone too far.

'Well, Captain Reid's not well ... he might be on a boat when he gets a blackout,' he said quickly. 'If he falls down somewhere the boat might take him away without knowing he's there —'

'I don't even know whether Captain Reid is on the jetty,' Jackson said. 'He might just be walking on the beach.'

'He's not,' said Docker, 'He's there.' He pointed over Jackson's shoulder. Swinging around, Jackson saw Reid emerge from behind a team of men unloading a sling on the jetty and wander over to a 44-gallon drum on which he sat, a forlorn and idle figure in the middle of the bustle.

'So he is,' said Jackson, quickly deciding his best course of action. 'You've come all this way to see what's going on, so let's see.' As Docker hesitated, he added sharply, 'Come on.'

When they reached Reid he merely nodded as Docker gave him one of his awkward salutes.

'Come down to get a breath of sea air?' Jackson asked conversationally. 'It's been bloody stifling up in the lines.'

Reid seemed calm, even apathetic. 'It's always cooler on the water,' he said. 'These boat crews dodge the worst of the heat but they lead a pretty risky life. The skipper told me that as soon as he's unloaded our stuff, he's got to take the rest of the cargo to Monabilla.'

Jackson's heart lifted in relief.

'I thought he was going back to the mainland.'

'He was originally, but there was a radio signal with new orders waiting for him when he arrived here. Now it's Monabilla and then Port Moresby. Well, we'd better get back to the unit, I suppose.'

Reid slipped off the drum and walked to his vehicle, looking old and tired.

15

Next morning breakfast for 82 Battery was tinned pilchards in a ghastly tomato sauce. Wilkinson doggedly ate all his, probably as an example. Mailey and the others ate some, Reid pushed his plate away.

'Hopeless,' he said.

'There could be some good news,' said Honeysett. 'Brigade says they're going to airlift in a bit of fresh meat.'

'If we can eat it before it goes bad,' said Taylor.

'Just eat fast. And more fresh vegetables are due to arrive soon in a couple of boats.'

'They don't frig about, those luggers,' Mailey said. 'The sails are just ornaments now. The Army gives them all the diesel they want and they turn on those big donks and keep going.'

'Where's this vegetable boat coming from?' Ramsay asked. 'I don't want any more yams.'

'I heard it's coming from the mainland,' Honeysett told him. 'Probably bringing turnips — ugh!'

'If you gourmets will excuse me,' said Wilkinson, standing up. 'I've got a pile of bumph to wade through. And I'll inspect K Troop gun positions before lunch. Could you persuade Gunner Tonkin not to hang his towel over the barrel again, Ted?'

'I'll persuade him,' said Mailey.

A boat duly arrived at Saruna two days later and 82 Battery was again called on to supply part of a big working party. J Troop had to contribute twenty men, to be at the wharf at noon. After lunch Jackson saw Reid chatting to a couple of signallers who were maintaining some field telephones and a few minutes later he strolled towards the patch of oil-stained grass called the vehicle park, climbed into his vehicle and drove away.

Soon afterwards Jackson, wondering what arrangements had been made about feeding the men at the wharf, went to the troop office to talk to Docker. He was not there or anywhere about. Jackson told the duty runner, who was reading a much-thumbed thriller on a bench outside the tent, to find him.

'The TSM is down at the wharf,' the runner said. 'Went down with the working party.'

'I thought Sergeant Long was detailed to take the party,' said Jackson, surprised.

'Sar-Major Docker took his place,' said the runner. 'He sent me to tell Sergeant Long just before the trucks left.'

A feeling grew on Jackson that he should go down to the wharf himself. Knowing how Wilkinson frowned on officers driving vehicles or riding motorcycles, he sent for his driver to make the trip look as normal as possible. The boat tied up at the jetty, he found, was old and small. Reid was not on the jetty but Docker was. He was pacing up and down beside the plank used as a gangway, six steps right and six steps left, looking, as usual, faintly absurd. If he had carried a sign reading, 'I am watching to see who goes on board this vessel,' his purpose could not have been more obvious. The J Troop men were humping hessian sacks, presumably full of vegetables, down to a waiting truck. A bombardier said to Jackson with hardly concealed sarcasm, 'We're OK, sir — the TSM is looking after everything.' Ignoring Docker, Jackson jumped aboard the boat at the bow and looked into the hold. It was almost empty. A tousled white man in filthy shorts and sandals was standing scowling.

'That's the skipper,' said a gunner, working on deck as hatch boss. 'He's dead keen to get out of here pronto to give him all night to travel in. Says he saw a bloody big Japanese destroyer on the way over. He's been yelling at everybody to hurry up.'

'Don't blame him,' said Jackson. 'Where does he go next?'

'Back to the mainland,' said the gunner. 'Broome, I think. Wish I could stow away. Eh, how about we go together, sir?'

'Can't,' said Jackson. 'Haven't got my toothbrush.'

He thought briefly of searching the lugger's primitive deckhouse, but he knew Reid could not have got past Docker. Jackson went ashore and looked for Reid's truck. He found it under the trees, but in a different place. Reid was sitting in the seat, arms folded around the steering wheel, staring intently through the windscreen at the lugger. His hands were trembling and the only parts of his shirt not black with sweat were his epaulettes. His haversack, bulging full, was on the seat beside him.

'Hello, Chris,' said Jackson.

'Hullo, George,' said Reid, not turning his head. 'I suppose Docker is still standing around as though he had an egg up his bum.'

'The men have nearly finished,' Jackson said. 'Let's go home.'

Still staring through the windscreen, Reid said, 'What did you think of the photograph?'

Jackson was unable to formulate a word.

At last Reid took his eyes off the jetty.

'I knew somebody had opened my haversack because the photograph had been put back face outwards. The somebody could only have been you. I deduced you were in a great hurry.'

'Yes,' said Jackson. 'I was in a great hurry. Docker was walking towards the truck. I opened your haversack to see if you had packed the kit you would need if you had . . .'

'Skipped off in one of these luggers? Very perspicacious of you. Do you know that Docker is watching me all the time?'

'I do,' said Jackson. 'He rigged the fatigue roster to come down to the jetty today.'

'I don't doubt it,' Reid said, almost dreamily. 'Yes, he's watching me. But you still haven't told me what you think of the photograph.'

Jackson could still find nothing to say. Reid sighed.

'Zoe understands about the mirror,' he said. 'I've written her giving full details. She knows how important it is to get to MacArthur. She knows ...' He seemed to fall into a reverie, from which he suddenly emerged with a jump, switched on the engine, slammed into gear and, shouting something incomprehensible, roared crazily away in a direct line through the trees towards the road.

Jackson drove back and saw Wilkinson. 'Can't you get Chris into hospital or something?' he asked. 'The poor bugger is raving. He's even worse with me than he is in the mess.'

'Well, there's no point in getting that self-important quack down again,' said Wilkinson, 'and I'm reluctant to have Chris taken to hospital by bodily force, which is about the only way he would go. Quite a problem, eh? You see, he's not actually incapacitated.'

'He's bloody certifiable.'

'And how!' Wilkinson agreed. 'I'll see what I can do.'

But two days later Reid missed breakfast, failed to appear for the troop's morning parade and later sent a gunner to ask Jackson to go to see him in his tent. He was sitting, at his table, on the little folding stool with the canvas seat and metal framework which he had carried with him first as a gun position officer and later as a troop commander.

'Ah, George —' he said, excitedly. 'Come in, come in!' He could not sit still. Jackson perched on the end of the stretcher. 'It's obvious the only way I'm going to get my calculations into MacArthur's hands is to take them back to Australia myself. But you know that already, don't you?'

Humour him, Jackson thought. 'Why don't you just ask for a movement order?' he said.

'Movement order!' Reid demanded. 'Do you think these boneheads here would ever give me permission to go even though I may be able to add something vital to our war effort. Have you thought of that? Something vital!'

'Have you thought that the skipper of a lugger might not be keen to take you?'

'Why not?' Reid half-shouted. 'Why not? The skippers

are civilians. Some are Islanders. They don't care if an army officer comes on board and says he's been ordered back to the mainland. That's not the problem. The problem is Docker. You saw what happened yesterday. I could have been on the boat that left last night if Docker hadn't buggered it up for me. Obviously I can't hang around the jetty any more, so this is where you come in.'

'Not much I can do,' said Jackson.

'On the contrary, you can do a lot. You can slip down to the wharf when the next boat is in. Have a word to the skipper and find out if he's going to Broome and warn him I'll be down. Then just pass me the word and I'll be away.'

'But Chris —' Jackson protested. 'Don't you realise you would be going absent without leave? Or even, well, deserting?'

'I don't care what you call it,' said Reid. He thumped his fist on the pile of figure-covered paper in front of him. 'These are what are important.'

Jackson looked out the open end of the tent. A group of gunners sitting under a tree were dozing through a lecture by an artificer from RAEME on the care of the recuperator. A small group had gathered around the command post assistant who was doing something with a book of range tables. The duty runner was deep in his whodunnit outside the troop office. This is home, Jackson thought. The world beyond seemed huge and frightening.

'I don't think you should do this,' he told Reid. 'I'm not knocking the importance of your ... your calculations, but you know you'd be court-martialled if you left here without a movement order. That's no way for a man with your military record to end up. As for me, I suppose I'm too conventional or something but I couldn't really see myself helping you to desert. I'm sorry if I sound priggish.'

'Ah,' said Reid, after a long pause. 'Well, you do.' He wiped his face with a handkerchief which was already a sodden ball, then opened it out and spread it over his knee.

'You know, George,' Reid said. 'I had hoped you would feel you owed me something.'

'I owe you a lot,' Jackson said.

'I mean a particular debt. I mean the little matter of my wife.'

The heat of a great flush raced up Jackson's neck.

'Exactly,' said Reid. 'You've been to bed with her. You've been fucking her.'

'Oh, for Christ's sake!' Jackson jumped up, horrified. 'Don't talk like that!'

'You don't like the word? I don't like the deed, but the fact is still there. That's why you owe me something. You've done me a grave wrong and you should do me a good turn to redress the balance. And you know what the good turn is.' Reid nodded with satisfaction as though he had produced a masterpiece of logical argument.

'How do you know about Zoe and me, anyway?' Jackson burst out.

'I didn't,' Reid said, 'or not for sure, until I saw your face a moment ago. Not that I hadn't suspected it. Zoe has a ... what shall I say ... an ardent temperament and in her letters she mentioned having you around to parties in an elaborately casual sort of way. Anyway, the point is simple. I want you to help me get to MacArthur.'

Jackson could not bring himself to look at Reid. He simply wanted to be by himself. Jumping down from the tent to the grass, he said, 'I'll think about it.'

'Don't think too long,' Reid called. He began to pound his closed fists on his knees in an oddly pathetic gesture. 'Don't think too long — there's another boat arriving in a couple of days. Don't let me down, George.'

Hiding in the solitude of his own tent Jackson vividly remembered Zoe lying exactly as she had in the photograph and he felt the beginning of an erection. Ashamed, he sat up, grabbed the old tin of Capstan Fine Cut in which he kept his Atebrin tablets and swallowed two; they might not make you impotent, he thought, but it was rumoured they quietened you down.

He put on his hat and headed off at random through the plantation, cringing every time he recalled how Reid had said, 'You've been fucking her.' Can it possibly be true that I should make amends to Chris by helping him skip? Jackson wondered. Surely that's just the product of a disordered mind ... or is it? Do people square things that way? He looked at his watch and saw it was only an hour to evening mess. He turned dismally back towards the lines, utterly confused.

He nearly stayed away from mess; he shied from the prospect of sitting near Reid, possibly jammed shoulder to shoulder. Reid, seen as Zoe's husband, had been a somehow non-sexual figure who merged with Reid, the troop commander. This was very different from post-photograph Reid, active sexual male. It revolted Jackson to think that he and this man had experienced with Zoe the same contortions, the same intertwining of hair, same sofa, same floor, same bed, same groaning cries, same small hand-towels, same stains. In the mess tent Jackson squeezed on the end of one of the seats. Reid, on the other end, was separated by two other officers who were arguing about football. Wilkinson was laughing at an old Irish joke Ramsay had told. In a lull Jackson heard Reid say excitedly, '. . . Just another example of military obtuseness. Why can't we take cameras on active service? I'm a photographer — why couldn't I take a picture of the plantation, say, as a landscape shot?'

'Rather have a picture of Greta Garbo,' said Honeysett.

'I'll have Jean Harlow,' said Mailey. 'Remember that white satin dress?'

'I've seen some really great footy photos,' rumbled Baby. 'Dunno how the cameramen seem to catch the action just at the right second.'

How in God's name did the subject of photography come up? Jackson asked himself. The recollection of Zoe in the print filled his mind and next moment a new scene presented itself to him as clearly as though it had come through a slide projector. Reid was standing beside Zoe as she lay on the bed. He, too, was naked and his big penis, which Jackson had seen often enough in various showers, was ready. Zoe, lifting her eyes to Reid's face as she had so often raised her eyes to his own, leaned slowly forward and opened her lips.

'You've played Union, haven't you, George?' Baby was asking him. 'Don't you reckon it's faster than League?'

Jackson found he had a mouthful of half-chewed food. He swallowed and said to Wilkinson, 'Could you excuse me for a moment, Major? I've come up without a handkerchief.' In the sticky night air outside he hurried away from the light streaming out of the tent. He was outside the unit lines before he stopped and made himself do deep breathing with arms raising ten times. He expelled his last breath and felt more able to think. It was obvious that he would not be able to endure living with Reid, perhaps — appalling thought — even having to hear him babbling on about Zoe. The answer was at hand, Jackson knew. His mind made up, he went back to the mess.

After the meal there was a poker game. Reid, once a regular and successful player, had given it up and this night he disappeared somewhere. Jackson played a few hands but found the constant, familiar, almost institutionalised banter a strain and excused himself. Walking through the lines he saw a light in the J Troop office. Reid was there, making notes out of some book by the light of a pressure lantern. Jackson went in.

'I've changed my mind,' he said. 'I think you should go.'

'And you'll organise it?' Reid asked eagerly.

'If I can,' Jackson said. 'If you're lucky, the next boat will head for Broome, too, and I may be able to keep Docker away. I'll see what I can do.'

'Wonderful!' said Reid. 'Wonderful!'

'No,' said Jackson. 'It's anything but wonderful. It's just practical, that's all.'

16

Four days later Jackson and Docker were in the troop office together when Honeysett came in, brisk and businesslike as ever. He put his clipboard on the table, wiped his steel-rimmed spectacles and said, 'Just making the rounds distributing news, good and bad. Let me see — Wilko said to let you know he is going to make a surprise inspection of all slit trenches around the tents at eleven hundred on Friday. He expects to see them all deep enough to protect every man in the tent.'

'We're not going to get any air raids, are we?' Jackson asked.

'My name's not Tojo,' said Honeysett. 'And we seem to have found a few spare shirts. If any of your blokes can produce a shirt genuinely rotted through, have him report to the quartermaster sergeant's tent this afternoon and see if he can talk Scrooge into issuing a new one. Now, about working parties. There's a boat due in tomorrow morning and we have to supply some bods.'

'Where's this boat coming from, sir?' Docker asked.

'Broome, I believe,' said Honeysett. 'It's got to be unloaded in twelve hours.'

'Why's that?' Docker asked.

'Apparently the boat's going straight back to the mainland and they want it to get a whole night's travel in the dark. Anyway, the idea suits us. Brigade wants the battery to have a working party on the dock from oh seven hundred to fourteen hundred and then a fresh mob from another unit will take over and clean everything up so the boat can get away by twenty hundred at the latest. Now, as to the bit that interests you, Sar-Major, J Troop's share of the battery working party will be fifteen men.'

Docker, staring fixedly at Honeysett, seemed hardly to hear him.

'Your detail will be fifteen men,' Honeysett repeated.

'Very good, sir,' said Docker, seizing a pencil and writing the figure down. 'You want them at the wharf at oh seven hundred.'

Jackson, forcing himself to sound casual, said, 'What's this great vessel bringing?'

'Food, I suppose,' said Honeysett. 'Or more paper for the duplicator at Brigade.'

'Do I understand we don't need any 82 Battery bods on the dock after two o'clock?'

'That's right,' said Honeysett. 'We get an early mark for once. Don't forget to tell the blokes about the shirts, will you?' He bustled out, looking at this watch.

Jackson glanced sideways at Docker. He was bent over his duties roster.

'You'll fix up the detail, Sar-Major?' Jackson asked.

'Of course, sir,' said Docker. 'I'll attend to everything.'

Jackson hesitated a moment but Docker still did not raise his head. Jackson went to look at the slit trenches. Reid seemed to be nowhere about. At midday mess he arrived late and left quickly. Jackson, going to his tent, found him pacing up and down inside it.

'I hear a boat's coming in,' he said.

'Tomorrow,' said Jackson. 'We have to supply a working party, but only until fourteen hundred. You should have plenty of time later to get aboard when there will be none of our men on the wharf to see you.'

'Tremendous,' said Reid. 'Tremendous. MacArthur is supposed to read maps in a flash. Shouldn't take him long to understand my drawings. My God, I'm looking forward to meeting him.'

'You understand,' said Jackson, 'that I will get you to

the wharf somehow but how you persuade the skipper of the boat to take you is up to you.'

'I've got a sort of ticket,' Reid said. 'I think we'll find it's valid.'

He picked up his copy of the blue-bound gunnery textbook and, holding it spine uppermost, shook it. A cascade of pieces of printed paper fell from between the pages. Jackson, looking more closely, saw they were Australian banknotes.

'There's a hundred quid there,' Reid said. 'That should convince a lugger skipper, eh?'

'For God's sake!' Jackson said. 'How long have you had these?'

'Long time,' said Reid. 'These are my poker winnings. I never thought they'd help us win the war.' He laughed delightedly. 'How about that, eh?'

Anxious to find something to do, Jackson called his driver and went out to the gun position where he poked about looking at equipment and chatting to the men. Two young gunners were playing chess. One, already a bachelor of science in palaeozoology, took his doctorate seven years later. 'Good-oh, sir,' he said. 'You're just in time to watch me do Roy. Silly bugger tried the queen's gambit declined.'

'There's some difference between talking and doing,' said the other player, a smooth-faced handsome boy from a rich family, who three moves later called 'Check'. Ten years later he was convicted of murder.

On Thursday the battery's working party left punctually if not happily for the wharf in charge of the K Troop TSM. At breakfast Reid appeared briefly, looking deadly ill, and ate a few ration biscuits smeared with some already melting tinned butter. He took the morning troop parade without any remarks to the men and went to his tent. Jackson called his driver and went to the wharf, ostensibly to check the working party, but in reality to try to guess what chance Reid had of getting on board the boat, which turned out to be a battered diesel schooner. The skipper, who looked half-Polynesian, was prowling nervously up and down the wharf wearing a pair of fatigue pants and an old pyjama jacket. 'Don't let these soldiers stand around scratching their arses, Captain,' he said. 'I want to be out of here soon after dark.'

Jackson went back to the lines. Neither Reid nor Docker was in the troop office tent. As Jackson walked to Reid's tent, he passed Docker's. Docker was inside, perched on the end of his bunk, staring at Reid's tent like a dog watching a rabbit burrow. Reid was in his tent, working at some figures on his pad of papers.

'The physics of light are marvellous!' he said to Jackson. 'I wish I'd paid more attention to them before the war.'

'Look,' said Jackson. 'Docker is watching you like a bloodhound. Don't you think you should give up this idea?'

'Certainly not,' said Reid expansively. 'Give it up just because of a halfwit like Docker? Like hell. The boat's here, isn't it? It's going back to Broome? Great! Did you get a chance to talk to the skipper?'

'Briefly,' said Jackson.

'Did he look the sort of bloke who might be amenable?'

'I'd say you'd find a way of convincing him. What worries me is how to get you out of our lines and down to the jetty without both of us ending in a court martial.'

Reid laughed excitedly.

'I've worked something out. You know that little hut, a couple of hundred yards down the road where I had the doubtful-looking cartridges stacked after the prem — the ones with the bags leaking cordite? I'll go to evening mess in the usual way and after it I'll slip down to the hut in the dark and wait there. If anything should go wrong . . . well, I went to take a look at the ammo. You get in your truck, pick me up at the shed, drive to the jetty and dump me there. What happens after that is up to me. You simply drive on to the gun position and show your face there. Nobody will even know about your little fifteen-minute side trip.'

'But I was at the guns yesterday,' Jackson protested.

'Sign of a conscientious officer, always in touch with his men,' said Reid. 'Good easy plan, eh?' He rubbed his hands in self-congratulation. 'OK — I'll see you at the hut at, say, nineteen thirty tonight. How about that?'

'Very well,' said Jackson. 'I'll pick you up at nineteen thirty. But for Christ's sake make sure Docker isn't walking one pace behind you.'

'I will,' said Reid. Ridiculously, he shook Jackson's hand and said, 'You are making a direct contribution to winning this war, George.'

At mess that night Reid arrived at the table sounding more obsessed than ever and Jackson noticed Wilkinson watching him closely. Although nobody was listening to him, Reid gabbled on and on about mirrors and light beams and the unwillingness of military high command to accept new ideas and then launched into a complicated story about the early rejection of the Gatling gun which became entangled with a diatribe about the bloodbaths created by the generals of the First World War. In the light of the pressure lantern, Jackson could see drops of sweat dripping down the sides of Reid's nose around his mouth and down to his chin. He mopped his face continually with his handkerchief. A couple of the other officers gulped down a few mouthfuls and escaped. Jackson looked at Reid, thinking, in disbelief, that this could be his last meal in the battery, perhaps his last in any military unit other than a hospital. At breakfast tomorrow, if things go as planned, Chris technically will have deserted and I am sitting here, knowing all about it, an accomplice . . .

'So who's on for a little slither tonight?' asked Wilkinson, who had calmly pursued his meal through all Reid's clamour.

'I might be in it,' said Mailey. 'It's time I won a bit back from Baby.'

'Bullshit,' said Baby, in organ-like tones. 'You've got a lot of my money.'

'How about you, Chris?' Wilkinson asked.

'Not tonight, thanks,' said Reid. 'I've got a bit of work to do.' He stood up and, lurching a little, made for the end of the tent. 'Work, work, work, there's no end to it. See you all tomorrow.'

'My God, Tim,' said Mailey. 'You'll have to get the

quack to do something about poor old Chris.'

'I'll have a talk to the Brigadier tomorrow,' said Wilkinson. 'Meantime — are you playing tonight, George?'

Jackson slowly put his mug of tea on the table and said, 'Yes, Major, I think I will. I've got to slip out to the gun position to fix up something first, but I'll be back after that.'

'We'll reserve you a seat.'

It's like the Last Supper, Jackson thought, except I can't quite tell who is Judas ... probably me. But now that he had committed himself with a half-truth which had come out with shameful smoothness, he felt almost relaxed. He stayed in the mess gossiping for half an hour and then left. There was no light in the troop office or Reid's tent. Jackson, feeling it would be an advantage to be seen in the lines as much as possible, strolled over to the battery office and chatted briefly to the battery sergeant major, who was playing euchre with the K Troop TSM, the battery clerk and a bombardier suspected of being over fifty. At twenty past seven Jackson wandered quietly into the vehicle park, climbed into GJ and drove slowly down the road towards the jetty. It was dark by now and his headlights soon picked up the tumbledown hut which the plantation workers had used to store tools before the war. Jackson stopped outside the hut and a moment later he heard boots scrape on the tailboard of the utility and the thump of somebody landing in the back.

'Is that you, Chris?' he called back, through the little square window in the canvas partition between the cab and the back.

'It's me,' said Reid. 'You're right on time.'

'Did anybody see you leaving?'

'I'm sure they didn't. I ducked out past that empty tent at the back. Come on, don't let's hang about here.'

Jackson jammed the truck into gear and drove towards the jetty.

17

Afterwards, Jackson realised that in the end he didn't say goodbye to Christopher Reid.

There was no clasp of the arm or wishes of good luck or even a handshake. It was only a few minutes' drive to the jetty which looked as though a squadron of fireflies was swarming over it. Ever since the night of the *Leeuwarden* sinking, unloading parties had struggled with boxes and bags by the light of anxiously shaded pressure lanterns or hand-held torches. As Jackson drove up a hoarse voice called, 'Get those fucking headlights out.' He turned on his parking lights. Jackson stopped the truck in the trees. Through the back curtain he heard Reid say, 'Great work, George. I'm going. You piss off to the guns as fast as you like.' Jackson heard boots scrape on the tailgate again and the sound of somebody landing on the roadway and he knew Reid had vanished in the darkness.

Jackson drove straight to the gun position, where, safely screened by the plantation from the sea, lights were on in the tents. He told the men he had come to make sure they had received the message about the available shirts, asked about the result of the chess game — a draw — drove back to the vehicle park, left the truck and walked towards the officers' mess tent. As he approached he heard Bolton say, 'Three kings! Beat that!' and the thwack as somebody hurled his cards on the table and some chuckles at an unheard remark.

He stepped inside the tent as Mailey said, 'Baby, you're the greatest tin arse since that character in *The Wizard of Oz*.' Jackson slid on the end of a seat. The familiar faces, the endless repetition of familiar catch phrases anaesthetised, at least for the moment, what he was feeling. He took a hand of cards. The rules of the mess game were immutable. The only variety played was straight five-card draw poker; the pot started at two shillings and could be increased to any amount by doubling. Honeysett, murmuring for the thousandth time, 'Nothing ventured, nothing won,' raised the pot to four shillings. Baby growling, 'I'm venturing,' raised it to eight. Wilkinson raised it to sixteen. Jackson waited for somebody to say, 'Oh, mother, your boy is nervous now,' or theatrically draw in his breath. Sure enough, Mailey, raising the pot to thirty-two shillings, said, 'Oh, mother, your little boy's getting nervous now.' Wilkinson, dealing, gave Jackson his cards, but before he could look at them Sergeant Major Docker appeared at the opening of the tent, hat on, and standing rigidly to attention, said, 'I'm sorry to disturb you, Major, but I should like to speak to Mr Jackson. It is important.'

Wilkinson looked quizzically at Jackson.

'I'll be right with you, Sergeant Major,' Jackson said. 'Just let me play this hand.'

'This is urgent,' said Docker.

'I'm out,' somebody said. 'I'll play your hand, George.'

Jackson went outside the tent. In the light coming through the canvas he saw Docker give him one of his idiotic salutes.

'What is it?' he asked.

'He's gone, hasn't he?' Docker said.

'Who's gone?'

'Reid's gone.'

'Do you mean Captain Reid?'

'You know who I mean,' said Docker. 'He's on that bloody ship without a leave pass. You know that.'

Jackson wondered how much of this could be heard inside the tent.

'I know nothing of the sort, Sergeant Major,' he said, 'and I advise you to get control of yourself.'

'He's deserting,' Docker said. 'He's deserting.'

'Stop this at once,' said Jackson, 'or I'll have to take action.'

'You take action! You officers are all the same — all stick together, all think your shit doesn't stink,' Docker half-shouted. 'I saw you drive out of the vehicle park and I went straight to Reid's tent. He wasn't there and he isn't anywhere in the battery area. I reckon you drove him down to the jetty.'

'I went to the gun position,' Jackson said. 'And if you go on like this I will place you under arrest.'

'What for?' said Docker. 'For reporting to you that Captain Reid is missing? I tell you what — I'll parade myself to Major Wilkinson and see what he thinks. He's inside the tent. I request an immediate interview.'

'You would do yourself more justice if you saw him in the morning.'

'No, I want to see him now. If you won't call him out, I will.' Docker strode to the opening in the tent again and said loudly, 'Major Wilkinson, I have an urgent request.'

All the card-players' heads swung towards Docker. Wilkinson, looking beyond Docker to Jackson, and seeing the consternation on his face, put down his cards and walked outside the tent.

'You're a bloody nuisance, Docker,' he said. 'Can't all this wait until morning?'

Docker, not looking at Wilkinson but at some point in the air over his head, said, 'I have reason to believe that Captain Reid, OC J Troop, is trying to leave this unit without permission. I believe he has gone to the jetty to stow away on the trading boat that is at the jetty now.'

'Are you boozed, Docker?' Wilkinson asked. 'Have you been on the jungle juice?'

'You know I'm a teetotaller,' said Docker.

'Do you understand what you're saying? Are you suggesting that Captain Reid is deserting?'

Docker's Adam's apple worked a couple of times, but he finally blurted out, 'Yes, sir, I think Captain Reid is on the boat now.'

'OK,' said Wilkinson. 'We'll settle this. We will look for Captain Reid and if we find him in the lines or at the guns or anywhere, Docker, I'll have your balls for a necklace. Understood? What do you know about this, George? Where did Chris go after mess?'

'As far as I know he went to his tent,' said Jackson. The lie came to him so smoothly he hardly noticed it.

Wilkinson put his head in the mess tent.

'Anybody here seen Chris since mess?' The surprised faces stared back at him. There was a chorus of 'No'.

Walking fast, Wilkinson led Jackson and Docker to Reid's tent, then to the troop office, the K Troop office and the battery office, from which he rang the gun positions of both troops. Docker, trailing sullenly along behind, said, 'You'll find him on the boat.'

'Very well, Docker,' said Wilkinson. 'We will look at the wharf and on the boat. We'll go down in your vehicle, George — you won't need your driver.'

Jackson, who had been feeling progressively more alarmed, looked at his watch. It was still only nine o'clock. The bloody boat might still be at the jetty, he thought, unloading is always slow without decent light. What if they find Chris aboard the boat? The idea terrified him; he felt like a man walking to the gallows. The three men got in the truck, Wilkinson in the front, Docker in the back. Jackson thought of wild schemes about pretending the engine would not start, or running off the road, but he knew Wilkinson would immediately detect any ruse like that.

Wilkinson said nothing on the way. Jackson, after silently rehearsing the words, said, 'We might find Chris wandering about getting a breath of air. He often walks about at night.' Wilkinson merely grunted.

Near the wharf they passed a couple of three-ton trucks, presumably fully loaded, going the other way. At the water-front the darkness was filled with muttered cursing and the gleams of torches, but on the jetty itself there seemed to be fewer flashes of light. A sudden hope filled Jackson; mur-muring, 'Back in a second,' he grabbed his own torch and hurried towards the wharf, half falling over a pile of bags on the way. Where the lugger had been there was now only blackness. Jackson shone his torch down the side of the jetty. It showed dark, still water. The lugger had gone.

18

'How long since the boat went?' Jackson asked a couple of men stumbling along pulling a hand trolley.

'Cast off about twenty minutes ago,' one man answered.

'Don't blame him,' said another voice in the darkness.

'You must have emptied the hold pretty smartly,' Jackson said.

'I dunno if we got it empty or not,' said the voice. 'The skipper was shitting himself to get away.'

Jackson walked off the jetty feeling almost light-headed with relief. He made himself stop for a moment and breathe deeply to get the elation out of his voice. Back at his vehicle, he said, 'The lugger has gone. We may find Chris wandering around somewhere in the dark here.'

'Be hard to find him in this,' said Wilkinson. 'Anyway, give the sergeant major your torch. Docker, you walk along the beach to the right of the jetty calling out Captain Reid's name. Then come back to the vehicle here.'

Docker took the torch and stalked away.

'I've brought a torch myself,' said Wilkinson. 'So we can have a look around, too. We could start with —'

'Jesus Christ, what's that?' asked a hoarse voice from somewhere nearby. 'That thing!'

Out to sea an elongated splash of light had started to dance along the water, perhaps half a mile offshore.

'That's a searchlight, of course,' said Wilkinson, calmly.

The splash became a tube of light boring through the blackness and a moment later it came to rest on what it was looking for, the lugger, just clearing the coastline. The men ashore could see the lugger's hull, its two masts, the big coachhouse just forward of the mizzenmast, all lit up like a stage setting. A moment later came the whang-whang-whang of the Japanese destroyer's guns. It fired three rounds. One seemed to miss, one carried away the mainmast and the third turned the whole boat into a huge gout of red and orange flame, shooting hundreds of feet into the air, in which pieces of the vessel could be seen twisting and turning. Almost at once came the noise of a huge detonation and a wave of hot air passed across the unbelieving spectators on the shore.

'Direct hit on something,' said Wilkinson. 'The boat must still have been carrying some ammunition.'

Jackson could hear the thwack-thwack of bits of wood and metal falling back into the sea. The destroyer's searchlight played on the pillar of twisting smoke and then came down to water level. Where a moment before there had been a ship, there was now nothing but some pieces of something in a pool of diesel fuel burning so strongly its flames danced on the faces of the men on the beach. The searchlight swung around to the jetty, passed over it with leisurely contempt, ranged around the foreshore for a moment and then, apparently finding nothing of further interest, began to travel along the ocean beach, slowly at first and then more rapidly, as the destroyer steamed away down the coast. Finally the light snapped out.

A crackling sound came from the pulverised remains of the lugger.

'Poor devils,' said Wilkinson. 'There'll be nobody left alive out there.'

By the light of the burning oil, he saw Jackson standing with his elbows dug into his stomach as though he had suddenly felt a devastating griping pain.

'For God's sake!' said Wilkinson. 'What's the matter?'

'Chris —' Jackson panted, 'Chris —'

Wilkinson seized him by one arm and spun him around. 'What about Chris?'

Jackson could only point to the flaming wreckage.

Wilkinson shook him violently.

'Was Chris Reid on that boat?'

116

'I think so,' said Jackson. 'I don't absolutely know.'

'He stowed away?'

'I think so,' said Jackson. 'That's what he intended.'

'I see,' said Wilkinson. His voice sounded, for once, weary and dispirited. Jackson tried to see his face but Wilkinson had his back to the flames.

'But you know how sick Chris had been,' Jackson said, desperately trying to palliate the offence. 'It's not as though Chris has been normal. And, look, Major, there's a bit more to this — about Chris getting down here, I mean. There's something I must tell you.'

'No, there's not,' said Wilkinson abruptly.

'But there is,' Jackson persisted. 'I'm most abysmally sorry but I must tell you.'

'No, you don't,' said Wilkinson.

A shape loomed up near him and Jackson saw it was Docker, his bony face stark with excitement.

'Did you see that?' he said. 'Like a fireworks show, wasn't it?'

'George,' said Wilkinson, 'give Docker the keys of your truck. Sergeant Major, drive straight back to our lines, find Captain Honeysett and ask him to send a message about what has happened to Brigade at once.'

'But don't you think I could be more useful here, sir. I mean —'

'Docker!' Wilkinson snapped. 'Get going!'

Docker, pursing his lips in prim disapproval, drew himself up and gave Wilkinson an insultingly elaborate salute.

'Very good, sir,' he said. 'But one thing is clear, isn't it? If Captain Reid can't be found anywhere we'll know where he was, won't we?'

Jackson did not grasp what he meant for a second, but then he lurched after Docker as he vanished into the darkness. 'Docker!' he shouted. 'Docker, I'll smash your whining face in!'

Wilkinson grabbed his arm and snapped, 'Calm down. Don't make everything worse.'

'That bastard hated Chris —'

'He hates all of us, but just calm down. Leave Docker to me. Understand?'

Some infantry officer had pulled things together on the jetty and a team of men were launching a rowboat to go out to the wreckage. Still holding George firmly by the arm, Wilkinson led him to a wooden crate of some sort and they both sat on top of it. For the first time that day Jackson thought of Zoe; he remembered her saying, 'You have no idea how well Chris and I get along together,' and in a thin, squeezed-out voice he hardly recognised as his own, he said, 'Oh, Christ, Major, I've been such a shit . . .'

'Take it easy,' Wilkinson said.

'But you've got no idea — it's not just here, tonight, it's more than that —'

'Shut up,' Wilkinson said, brutally. 'Shut up, will you?'

A moment later he added, more kindly, 'Do you know the really nasty thing about a war? It exposes everybody's weaknesses. Physical, mental, moral — if it goes on long enough, I mean. Not so much in the Army. The Army is a sort of corset that can help men control weakness. But back home — it's not just the blackmarketeering and the draft dodging and the job grabbing; it's women, too.'

'Major,' Jackson said. 'Major, listen —'

Wilkinson ignored him.

'Sometimes people think they can make everything all right again by blabbing out confessions, usually to the people who will be most hurt by what they hear. I've always thought that's a particularly shitty trick — for God's sake, if you give yourself a heavy pack, the least you can do is carry it yourself.'

Somebody turned on the headlights of a truck and in their beam Jackson saw the boat being clumsily rowed towards the pool of flickering oil. 'I don't envy them,' said Wilkinson, softly. 'They won't like what they find.'

He jumped off the crate and said, suddenly brisk, 'Bugger all this philosophising, George. We'd better have a conference.'

'A conference?' Jackson repeated, hardly comprehending. An immense weariness was creeping over him.

'You bet,' said Wilkinson. 'Have you thought that what's happened tonight is going to result in a court of enquiry?'

'No, I hadn't.'

'Well, think about it now. The first thing the court will want to know is how an artillery officer without a movement order was on a boat heading for the mainland.'

'Of course,' Jackson muttered. 'Of course.'

'Have you ever heard of an AIF officer being court-martialled for desertion?'

'No,' said Jackson. 'No.'

'Neither have I,' said Wilkinson. 'Must be bloody awful for the bloke's friends and family, if he's found guilty, whether he's alive or dead. And aiding and abetting desertion is almost as serious.'

Jackson felt too tired to answer.

'Yes, this question of no movement order is certainly going to upset the court,' Wilkinson went on conversationally, 'but we all know poor old Chris had gone batty with the malaria, eh? After all, I got the quack down to see him once. I'm sure the court will ask why I didn't have him taken to hospital in a blanket, and I'll get a nasty rap on the knuckles, but that's my worry. The important fact is that Chris had become very confused lately. I think it's obvious he wandered down to the jetty after mess, thinking our blokes were still unloading, and he fell asleep somewhere on the bloody boat and got carried out to sea.'

Jackson nodded dully. He seemed to have been at the jetty for a year.

'George!' said Wilkinson, sharply. 'Do you agree that's what must have happened?'

'That's right,' said Jackson.

'Of course, Docker may make all sorts of wild accusations when he gives evidence, but it's no secret that he had an irrational dislike of Chris.'

'That's right,' said Jackson again. He merely wanted to sleep now.

Wilkinson touched him on the shoulder.

'How old are you, George — twenty-three?'

'Twenty-two.'

'Christ,' said Wilkinson. He sighed and finally said, 'You look wrung out. Piss off back to the unit and get some rest.'

'I'm OK,' Jackson said automatically.

'Come on, I'll stick around here in case somebody's needed. Hitch a ride with one of the trucks there.'

'I'll walk,' said Jackson. 'It's not far.' He slid awkwardly off the crate.

'See you tomorrow, then,' said Wilkinson, turning away into the darkness towards the end of the jetty.

Jackson tramped away through the edge of the plantation. He bumped into a tree trunk, fell on one knee and got to his feet again. It seemed a long time before he found the road and headed towards the unit, mechanically putting one foot in front of the other. There was no traffic at all on the road and its potholed earth surface was merely a strip of something a little lighter than the cliffs of darkness on either side of it, striated vertically by the trunks of palm trees.

After a while Jackson heard somebody talking to him. It was not Reid, though, but Shannahan.

'What ho, Malvolio!' Shannahan said. 'In the end we never did fire at anything over open sights, did we?'

'I killed him,' Jackson said. He stumbled over a pothole and nearly fell again. 'I wanted to get him off the island.'

'Here,' Shannahan said. 'Don't forget Wilko is going to inspect the slit trenches tomorrow.'

'Is it tomorrow?' Jackson asked.

'Better have a quick look at them first, eh?'

'I suppose I'd better.'

Shannahan chuckled.

'Bloody Army,' he said. 'Never stops.'

'Bloody Army,' Jackson agreed.

He came to a fork in the road just visible in the darkness and down the side track he saw the lights of the 82 Battery tents. I'm nearly home, he thought. As he shambled on he heard another, fainter, voice replacing

Shannahan's. He strained to hear the jumble of words. Somebody seemed to be shouting, 'Troop target, charge three, zero, left, four degrees,' and finally Jackson realised that the voice was probably his own.